Summer Island Hope

Ciara Knight

Reader Letter

Dear Reader,

This story is near and dear to my heart since many of the issues the heroine faces I myself endured during my third pregnancy. I hope this book brings light to some of the challenges parents face when having children with unique needs. Since I don't want to spoil the story before you've read it, I'll just share that a lot of what is written is first-hand knowledge in regards to health care, special needs, and the challenges parents and practitioners face. However, real life is sometimes not entertaining, so after receiving notes from editing, I toned down some of the specialist comments to be more reader-friendly. I shed some tears and laughed aloud while writing this book as I hope you will, too.

Most of all, I hope you enjoy Katherine Stein's story.

Sincerely,

Ciara

Summer Island Hope
Book III
Friendship Beach Series

Cover art by Yocla Cover Designs
Edited by Bev Katz Rosenbaum
Copy Edit by Jenny Rarden
Proofreading by Rachel

Created with Vellum

Chapter One

THE VIDEO CHAT shrilled a warning at Kat that Wes wanted to chat. Chat about her plans to return to Chicago —to him.

Energy pulsed through her like it normally did before she entered a courtroom at the start of a trial. She set her cup of chamomile tea to the side, brushed on her best faux-smile, and clicked answer.

The screen erupted with the love of her life, a handsome man with bright-blue eyes that Kat imagined resembled the color of the sky in heaven. Her heart fluttered. She'd missed him so much. They were apart often, sometimes for months at a time, but for some reason, the last few weeks had been torturous.

"Hi, my love. What time should I plan to pick you up tonight?" Wes's voice came through vibrant and enthusiastic, like his attitude toward life. The man could make Bozo the Clown look depressed.

"I'm good." Kat struggled with her real answer that would pop his happy balloon. Their relationship had grown to a new level during their vacation to a private island in the South Pacific almost two months ago. He'd spoken of taking time off to have the freedom to travel the world with her, and she'd been caught up in his enthusiasm. But now that she faced the reality of time off from her practice, she realized she couldn't be who he wanted—a free spirit who'd make a good wife.

"What is it, gorgeous?" He always knew when something troubled her. Since their first date, he'd been able to read her like no one ever could. She'd always prided herself on her ability to remain blank—it served her well when facing jurors when she thought her client could be guilty. Of course, he'd been an attorney, too. Her silent partner while he ran his business until his software solutions company took over his life.

"It's just that..." Kat dared a glance at the screen that framed his jet-black hair, strong jawline, and expectant gaze. She hated to hurt his feelings, but she'd seen how secrets tore lives apart every day in the courtroom. They'd made a vow to always be honest and up front, and it had worked for them for several years.

His ear-to-ear smile wavered but recovered. "You can tell me anything."

Turmoil spun, churning her desire to be with him with her fear of facing the truth, that she didn't believe in marriage. How could she after witnessing her own parents' misery? Like dropping an unexpected fact onto a jury, she said, "About tonight? I'm not going to make it."

He shrugged. "No worries. I can get you tomorrow. I've got some news I hope you'll be excited about."

Kat steadied herself, trying to remain focused despite the exhaustion threatening to put her in bed again. She rubbed her stomach, trying to settle the queasiness she'd struggled with the last few days. She needed to find the strength to tell him she had second thoughts about getting married, but the last week or two she'd been fatigued and wanting to sleep all the time. A fact that had driven her to the internet to check her symptoms, only to discover the worst new possibility. Probable menopause.

When had she gotten so old?

She inhaled a deep breath and focused on breaking the heart of the man she loved. "I bought my parents' house. I've got some details to figure out before I can fly back." There, she'd said it, and based on his deflating posture, she knew he'd listened.

"You bought your parents' place? The one you said was lonely except the occasional visit when they'd fly into town for holidays? The house you couldn't wait to escape the second you graduated high school?"

"Yes," she said, but the weight of hurting him drove her to say more. She'd learned a long time ago never to share more information than necessary when facing an opponent, but somehow Wes always drew out all her thoughts. "But it's a good investment. Home prices on the island are skyrocketing."

He shrugged. "Sounds like a solid idea."

Kat sat back in her father's old desk chair and eyed the screen. "You're not upset that I didn't tell you about this before I did it?"

"No. Why would I be? We're not married."

Ouch. A sting shot through her like an injection of acid. "Right, not married," she mumbled. Happy feet danced in her belly at the thought of being Mrs. Weston Knox. Yet, the promise of happily ever after was a lie.

"Unless you've changed your mind and you'll make an honest man out of me?" He winked, his dark lashes accentuating his playfulness that always stirred her up inside, but this time it only churned the nausea.

She lifted the cup to her mouth, but the smell warned her not to sip the beverage, so she put it back on the coaster and longed to return to bed. "I just thought you'd be upset because you've been pressuring me for the last two years to travel the world with you, to be free of all entanglements, and a house—"

"A house is a good investment, especially in Florida. Besides, we don't have to live there. You can have a management company handle all the business, repairs, and rentals." Wes ran a hand through his thick hair, flipping it back to the one side in that underwear-model way of his. How could he look so young while her body decayed from age? Menopause was a cruel, ruthless enemy.

Kat swallowed her anxiety. Why was it that she could argue in front of Supreme Court judges, take on the most acclaimed attorneys, but when it came to looking into Wes's eyes, she would tremble and her knees would go weak? Never had a man ever stolen her words until he entered her life. "I thought maybe we could use this as a vacation home more than a rental property. You know, since I've reconnected with Jewels, Trace, and Wind."

Wes scrubbed his jaw as if to consider her words. "Ah, the infamous Friendsters. Of course, I should've realized you'd want a place there. No worries, I get it. We'll plan to stay there for a few weeks a year. It's about time I met them, you know."

Kat relaxed at the sight of his sexy eyebrow raise and offered a playful smile. "You'll like it here. It'll remind you of our recent vacation."

His eyes widened, and his lips curled into a mischievous grin. "I like that place already."

She giggled like a five-year-old instead of the fifty she was. "It's inspired me to remember our conversation at sunset our final night on the beach." The one where she'd told him to ask her to marry him again. Promising she'd say yes this time.

"Now I really can't wait for you to return. And that will be...?" he asked.

Her stomach rolled over and died. "I don't know. I want to stay a little longer. I've been working remotely, and I don't have any court dates for months at this point." Coward. She needed to tell him she didn't think she could take that much time away, to give up everything she'd worked so hard to achieve for a man. Not even for him. She'd never be her mother.

"Months?" He shook his head. "Nope, no way. Pull up your calendar."

"What?"

"Do it right now," he insisted.

She picked up her phone, and after she entered her authentication codes, she brought up her personal calendar. "Okay."

"Look back to when we took our trip and count the days," he ordered more than asked.

She did as instructed, counting through the dates marked pink for nail appointments, blue for hair appointments, red for period...wait. Her nails tap, tap, tapped over fifty days with no more red dots. Her throat went mid-life dry. "Fifty," she mumbled through a haze.

"Now, look at tomorrow's date."

"Yeah." Her mind still hung on the fact it had been fifty days since their trip and over fifty days since her last period. Obviously, the big beacon of old age flashed ahead.

Menopause. Menopause. Menopause.

"And put in *Wes arrives with flowers and open arms at the front steps of your new house* at two in the afternoon."

"Okay." Kat still stared at the date. Her period had never been late. She'd trained it the way she'd trained her clients to obey her instructions, the way she'd trained her friends to listen to her guidance, the way she'd trained Wes to be a good boyfriend. She shook her head. It was ridiculous. It was all the stress of buying the house, of reuniting with her Friendsters. She didn't know what to do, how to think, to breathe. All she knew was she needed time to figure this out on her own. What the next stage of their relationship would be. "You can't make it tomorrow. You run a company."

"Remember, freedom? I'm the owner and we have no kids and no pets, so no problem. We can live our life the way we've always wanted. Free and fun. And that's part of what I want to talk to you about. I'm ready to take our next big step and cut some more ties so we can run away together. Just the two of us. On another private island beach somewhere exotic and wonderful."

"Okay," Kat mumbled, still staring at the blasted number on the calendar. It had to be wrong.

"You alright?" Wes asked, leaning into the camera as if he'd see something more clearly.

"Um, sorry. I'm distracted." Old age. What a slap in the face. When did she get this old? "The Friendsters just showed up. I have to run."

So much for not lying.

"No sweat. I'll see you tomorrow and the day after that and every day after that. It'll be just the two of us living on love," he said in a sappy commercial voice.

"Love you, too." She clicked End faster than a button on *Family Feud.*

No. No. No.

It couldn't be true. She was overreacting. Her fingers tapped over the keys.

Exhaustion, nausea, moody, fifty.

The results filled her screen.

Pregnancy.

No. Not possible. She was on the pill. The doctor had changed her prescription, but she was sure it still worked. The search had to be wrong. She retyped her symptoms in a new order.

Fifty, exhaustion, nausea, moody.

Geriatric pregnancy.

The words struck her with a one-two punch.

Perhaps she'd hit menopause and it messed with her cycle. She felt like she was a sixteen-year-old facing a prom night mistake. Was this what Jewels felt like all those years ago? Poor girl.

Kat pushed from the desk and paced the study with the ornate wood paneling, down the hallway that led to the grand staircase, to the big empty gourmet kitchen, to the lanai, around the pool, downstairs to the staff quarters, upstairs to the viewing deck. No matter where she went, though, the word followed. She was late and moody and nauseated and lost.

And pregnant?

Wes held the Montblanc pen Kat had given him for Christmas two years ago. It hung over the line as if he would be signing over his soul instead of selling his company. The morning light scattered around the high-rise, splintering golden hues.

All night he'd reviewed his reasons for why he'd even entertained the idea of giving up his life's work for a woman. He'd done nothing but work for the last twenty years to build his empire, working as a lawyer while starting his company then full-time at nothing but his business, only to sell it now. But in the last five years, he'd barely been able to see Kat when both their schedules lined up, which happened about as often as a total eclipse.

Since he'd met her, his values, needs, and desires had changed. Now, he longed for his workday to end to catch a glimpse of her passing in the evening on her way to her home office to work.

He touched the pen tip to the paper. "Do it, man," he said aloud as if to order his body into submission. There was no reason to hang on to his company. He'd taken Facile from local attorneys to national to global. Now, he'd grown the software company as far as he could, and it wasn't like he had an heir to take over running it. No children had been agreed upon from date one with Kat. One thing that had worked between them from the start. He'd sworn never to have children, and since Kat was fifty and he was fifty-two, it wasn't an issue with her anymore. No one in their right mind would have a kid at this age.

His hand scribbled the W, but he hesitated. "Do it for Kat." There was nothing more he wanted in life now than to enjoy the money he'd made, and selling his company afforded him that luxury. The idea of sweeping sweet Kat away from work to enjoy life together. Besides, he had some exciting ideas of what to do next. He'd thought about what came next in his early retirement. He wanted to pass on his legacy of knowledge and use his connection and money to do something meaningful. He'd have time to flesh out how to do that now. The idea of Kat and new possibilities urged him to scribble the rest of his signature. Before he gave it another thought, he stuffed the contract into the folder and set the pen on top.

Now that that was done, he needed to grab his stuff and head to the airport, making one stop along the way. He snagged his suitcase and rolled on out of their top-floor apartment overlooking the city—a view they'd both fallen in love with when they'd bought the place, but now he wanted to see oceans and mountains and Kat in a bikini.

He took the elevator to the lobby and paused at the front desk to speak with Thomas. He was more than a doorman. He'd become a friend over the years. A friend he'd miss. "Hey man, how's it going?"

"Good. Bundle up. The hawk is flying." He pointed to the large-screen TV overhead that said, *Baby, it's Cold Outside. Chiberia is coming.*

"Thanks for the warning. I won't miss these temperatures."

"Where you off to?" Thomas picked up a pen and opened his old-fashioned journal.

"Summer Island, Florida, where sun will warm my skin and Kat will warm my heart." Had he really just said that? Wow, he'd become cheesy.

"I sense something special going on in that brilliant brain of yours."

Someone opened the front door, sending a bitter blast through the lobby. Thomas tightened his coat, and Wes buttoned his up, wrapped the scarf around his neck, and plopped his hat on his head. Perhaps his next venture could be to help Thomas better his life beyond standing in a cold doorway. Although, the man always appeared happy. Besides, he wanted to do something meaningful, beyond business, busy work, and boosting one man's opportunities. He shook off his spinning thoughts and focused on the now. "I'm off to pick up something special."

"The ring? You going to finally propose?" Thomas rounded the front desk and removed his glove, holding his hand out to Wes. "Good luck, man. As my daughter would say, you two deserve a romcom happily ever after."

Wes shook his hand. "I agree. And I'm going to head out to make that happen. I don't know how long we'll be gone, so if you don't mind—"

"I'll keep an eye on your place, even check for any winter pipe issues daily."

"Great, thanks."

Wes dared the icy chill, but despite the burn on his cheeks, his body remained warm—warm with the idea that he'd be with Kat and engaged by the end of the day. And if she was willing, back on their private island getaway by the end of the week. He snuggled his cashmere scarf—the one Kat had given him last Christmas—and rolled his small suitcase behind him. Nothing would stop him from picking up the ring.

He only hoped that she'd say yes this time. New ring, new proposal, new life.

She'd been a little distant the last week, but chatting over text and video calls was impersonal at best. They needed quality time together, so he managed the salted sidewalk to the jeweler's, where he'd personally designed the ring.

Keith, their regular salesman, opened the red box with gold leaf etching to reveal the five-carat teardrop with two rounds of small diamonds encircling the center stone. Classic, beautiful, elegant—a perfect ring for Kat. "Thank you." He took the ring box, wrapped in a gold bow, tucked it into the inside pocket of his jacket, and raced to the airport, catching an earlier flight.

The three-hour trip dragged like the opera he'd taken Kat to in an attempt to impress her on their third date. To his relief, she'd fallen asleep halfway through, one of the many reasons he loved her. That and their shared dream of living life to the fullest, free and happy together. He'd never met a woman willing to forego family for fun.

He fidgeted the entire flight and gripped the wheel tightly in the rental car, realizing he didn't have a plan to propose. Perfect ring, check. Perfect woman, check. Perfect life, check. Perfect proposal? Nada.

The bumpy road into town jolted his nerves, and the tiny buildings with people waving at him made him uneasy. *Come on, man. Get it together.*

He'd planned on taking her to their favorite restaurant in Chicago, but when she'd changed her plans to stay, he knew he needed to come up with a new idea. Sunset on the beach? Too cliché for Kat. Romantic dinner at a fancy restaurant? He eyed the shack to his left and the tiny, weathered wood of a place called Cassie's Catch on the right that looked like a local fish dive.

His nav shouted at him to turn left and warned that her home would only be a few blocks away. Perhaps he'd just be waiting at the front door on one knee with the ring held out when she answered. Yes, that could work. Not too fancy but a statement that he couldn't wait another minute to make her his wife. She'd say yes this time, he knew, because they'd talked about it when they were away together. He'd made it all through his thirties and halfway through his forties, never thinking about proposing, only to make this the fourth proposal to the same woman.

He pulled into the drive of a massive mansion-style home with a wrought iron fence and rust-colored Italian roof tiles. So much for a little summer cottage. It didn't matter. They had the money. Whatever Kat wanted, he could give her, and she deserved everything.

The hot, sandy air beat on his skin, and sweat pooled at his collar before he even opened the back door to retrieve the ring from his coat pocket. He'd known it would be hot here, but this felt like Hades at high noon as Thomas would say.

With his pulse patting faster than his feet on the front stone walkway, he raced up the few front steps to the oversized iron double doors. One, two, three deep breaths and he rang the bell, stepped to the side, hopefully out of camera range, knelt down on one knee, holding up the ring, and waited.

And waited.

And waited.

And waited.

Chapter Two

Lunch at Jewels's usually smelled divine, especially when her daughter, Bri, cooked. She had a gift for the culinary arts. If her writing career didn't pan out, Kat thought she'd nudge Bri toward being a chef. The aroma of spicy Tex-Mex churned her stomach and burned her throat with rising acid. Ugh. When would the nausea stop?

She'd given it tremendous thought and decided she must've picked up a bug on top of the beginning of menopause. It made the most sense.

She halted at the edge of the front door and turned her head away from the open window to get one more deep breath of cleansing sea air. Houdini, their pet ferret, chittered at her, his nose poking into the wire mesh between the open green window slats. "Hey, boy."

He squeaked a reply, and the door flew open. "Why you standing out there?" Wind stood in her floral chiffon cover over her bathing suit.

If Kat was pregnant—which she didn't think she could be, considering she was on the pill and she was too old—bikinis were a thing of her past. Along with her hopes and dreams and plans and...Wes. Her heart sank like the Titanic had hit Antarctica.

"Kat, you okay?" Wind swept out, put an arm around her, and whisked her inside.

Houdini hopped on Trace's sun-kissed blonde hair and landed at the edge of the side table. Trace swatted at him playfully. "Told you, not on my head." She ran her fingers through her hair, taming the frays. "What's got you ghost white?"

Kat blinked at Trace and forced words to form. "Nothing."

"Drop everything. Friendervention alert," Wind called to the kitchen.

The smell of hot peppers and an inquisition made Kat want to run. She eyed the door, but Trace hopped off the couch and blocked her way out. That girl had a spring in her step since she'd started dating Dustin Hawk. "Don't even think about making an escape."

"Me?" Kat wanted to fall on her knees and have a good cry, but she hadn't done that since her mother had told her in the sixth grade that people didn't care about tears, they only respected strength and determination.

"Trace is right. You do look pale, darling. Here, sit." Jewels pulled out the bistro chair, and Bri stuck a glass of water in her face.

She needed to stay hydrated since everything that went down the last few days kept coming up.

"Thanks." Kat took a sip, but when Bri returned to the stovetop and opened the pot lid, sending a rush of peppery beef that attacked her nose, she fled to the bathroom for round number four of praying to the porcelain god. When nothing was left in her stomach, she blotted her face with a damp washcloth, took in a deep breath of eucalyptus soap, and returned to the living room to face four pairs of expectant eyes.

Wind snapped into motion first. "You poor girl. You sick?"

Trace fluffed a pillow, and if Kat didn't know better, her rough and tough friend actually showed concern. The only girl Kat thought of as stronger and more emotionless than herself.

"Don't make a fuss. I'm fine." Yet she gladly sat and closed her eyes for a moment. "It's just a stomach bug." Yep, that had to be it. A virus that attacked women who missed their period.

"You sure that's all it is?" Jewels asked in that motherly tone of hers. "I mean, you've been a little off the last week or so."

"Off? No I haven't."

The girls all did that *look at each other* thing. "Stop. Fine. I've been a little off, but I've had the purchase of my parents' house and you all doing your *falling in love* thing. Wind's been running off, and Bri's had her little reunion with her blast-from-the-past boyfriend."

"Sure. That's what has you flushed and pale, all within minutes." Wind picked up the fan she'd been given from some Asian royal family who saw her in a play on Broadway and waved it in Kat's face.

"Not to mention that nausea. Maybe you should see a doctor," Trace said, tucking one leg under her and propping Houdini on her lap, stroking his fur. But he didn't stay. Instead, he ran over and curled up on Kat, resting one paw on her belly.

Jewels sat on the driftwood coffee table in front of her. "Hmm."

Kat flinched. "Hmm, what?" She scooted the all-knowing Houdini from her lap. He shook his head and ran up the board to his shelf and looked down on her in judgment.

"Nothing, just that you're flushed but pale, sick to your stomach, and irritable."

"I'm not irritable," she shouted in a *too loud for an inside* voice. "Much."

Jewels took both her hands and held them tight. "Hon, is there any chance you could be pregnant?"

Wind laughed so hard she fell off the arm of the chair. "Pregnant? We're passed that age."

Kat shot her a prosecuting gaze.

"Oh." Wind covered her mouth with both pointy peach nail hands. "No. Oh hon, I didn't mean that."

"You're going to have a baby?" Trace asked in a too-quiet whisper, as if the world found out, lightning would strike them down.

Houdini chattered as if to say *I tried to tell you all.*

Kat pushed up from the chair, knocking knees with Jewels, ignoring the dizziness that threatened to take her to the ground from lack of calories. "I don't know that I'm pregnant. I'm sure I'm just ill. Some sort of weird virus or something. I'm on the pill, and well, I've been on it forever. Why would I get pregnant now? It isn't possible. It's a virus."

"Have you missed a period?" Wind blurted.

"I'm menopausal." Kat spat out the bitter words.

"Oh my gawwwwd, you're pregnant," Wind shouted, as if the people in the arctic needed to know.

"No, I'm not. Pill, menopause, remember?" Kat huffed. "Right, Jewels?" She looked to the only woman in the room who had ever had a baby.

"Probable no, possible yes," Jewels said, her hand resting on Kat's back. "No matter what, we're all here for you. You know that, right?"

Kat scooted away from the huddle of friends. "Yes." She drifted around the room, wishing she knew but fearing finding out.

Houdini bolted along the shelf to the other side of the room. For once, that strange little rodent had helped. She did feel better unloading on her friends. Her mother would be disappointed in her for needing someone to help her through any circumstance. Heck, Mother would be disappointed in her being pregnant. Of course, she could be disappointed in Kat for breathing, so what did it matter?

"Have you told Wes?" Trace asked.

"No. He's made it clear he never wants children. I'd be on my own with this."

"Not alone." The girls surrounded her in a friend circle. "We've got you, girl. But you do need to tell Wes. Even if he says he doesn't want kids, he has a right to know," Bri said, as if the girl who was eighteen years younger would know how she felt at this moment. Kat knew she meant well, though. They all did.

"I'll tell him if there's anything to share," she snipped.

"Then let's go get a test." Jewels slid away and snagged her purse from the hanger on the wall near the kitchen.

The clock struck one, and Kat knew she had a way out. "I can't go right now. Wes's coming to visit. He should be here any time. I need to get home."

Wind sashayed between them. "I'll go let hunky man into your place, no worries. I'll tell him you got caught up with some client or something. Don't worry. I'm a good actress." She winked.

"No way. You're not getting near him. You don't keep secrets."

Wind held her hands to her chest. "I'm deeply hurt."

Kat eyed the clock. "I've got an hour. I'll run to the drugstore and then to the house. I'll do the test later."

"I'll go with you to get it. We should probably hit the shop closer to Cocoa Beach if you don't want the entire town to know by dinnertime. The Small-Town Salty Breeze Line is alive and awaiting the latest and greatest gossip."

"Right, good point." Kat checked her watch. "Fine, let's go."

"I've got a meeting, but call me and let me know." Bri returned to the kitchen. The girl knew when she was welcome to be part of the friend group and when she didn't fit in, and right now, she was too young to understand what Kat faced.

Kat headed for her car, but Wind snatched the keys. "I'm driving."

"No, I'm driving." Trace stole the fob from Wind.

Kat took it back and faced Jewels. "You drive?"

"Sure."

They all climbed into the Lexus convertible she'd picked up a week ago. Wind and Trace sandwiched into the small back seats without complaint.

"Hey, this feels like the road trip we always talked about taking," Kat said, imagining her troubles away. The problem was she'd always been better at doing than imagining. That was more Wind's thing.

Jewels drove up Sunset Blvd and hung a left to head toward Cocoa Beach.

At the edge of town, the sea breeze swept through Kat's hair and calmed her stomach, so she relaxed for a few seconds.

She shoved the idea of a baby from her mind. It was ludicrous. Impossible. "Let's do that." She pulled her phone out of her purse. "Let's drive up the coast. I can take some time off in a few months. Let's say the second week in May."

The car came to an abrupt stop. Wind squealed like a little girl. Trace grunted. Kat saw the sign.

Jewels leaned out the left side of the car as if to see what was going on ahead. "I forgot about the construction."

"I hope we can make it there and back in an hour. Maybe I should postpone this trip until tomorrow. I'm feeling better. The nausea's gone." A baby, really? The idea was ludicrous. Impossible. "We can go back to my house and start planning our trip together. It's long overdue." Ignoring the dozen or so undoubtedly work-related text messages, she danced her thumbs over the keys and entered *Girls road trip* into her calendar.

She caught Trace's you're-in-denial expression in the rearview mirror. "What? I'm not pregnant. There's no way. I'm telling you. I've been on the pill forever and never had an oops. Ever."

A nagging voice in her brain answered before any of the girls did: *But there's a first time for everything.*

Anything was better than facing her friend's accusatory look, so she decided work would be a good distraction. She touched the text app to discover several messages from Wes.

Caught an earlier flight. See you by one instead of two. XOXO

"Turn the car around," Kat ordered.

"You're not escaping this that easily." Wind patted her shoulder.

"No, seriously. Wes's already here. Look." She held up her phone so Trace and Wind could see the text.

"She's not kidding. Abort Operation Baby Check and head to her place. Time to meet the creator of the bun in the oven."

"Stop, Wind," Jewels scolded.

Kat didn't have the energy to be mad at Wind.

Jewels leaned over and whispered, "You know she only means to cheer you up and distract you, not to be mean."

"I know, and I appreciate it," Kat said, and she did. "All this will be over soon. We'll all have a good laugh tomorrow as we sip margaritas on my rooftop."

Jewels managed to go off the side of the road and whip around to head back to the house. "I'll take you home, and then we can walk back to my place. It's a nice day for a stroll."

"Thanks." She took in a lungful of air and trusted that everything would be okay. She knew with her friends by her side, she could face anything.

They made it back to Kat's place in record time.

"There's Mister Hunkamungas." Wind took off her seat belt and stood up in the back of the car and whistled.

Trace yanked her down but then leaned forward. "What's he doing on your front porch?"

"Stop the car. Stop." Kat stared across the street at Wes down on one knee. A magical and terrifying sight when she knew she couldn't say yes. "I forgot I told him when we were away together last month that I would marry him if he asked me again. I can't reject him. Not for a fifth time."

"Five?" Wind grumbled. "I'd take once."

"I can't say yes. Not until I know." She rubbed her

belly, and an unwanted warmness spread through her abdomen.

She glanced up at Wes again, and her muscles seized and her head spun. "Oh my God. No." Kat covered her eyes and ducked. "I can't do this right now. I can't."

Chapter Three

Wes's knee throbbed, but he remained on the ground, hoping and praying the love of his life would open the door and squeal with delight. Okay, Kat wasn't the squealing type, but the simple word "yes" would suffice.

Rapid footsteps raced up behind him, and he turned to see a woman he recognized as Julie Boone from pictures he'd seen—Jewels, as Kat called her. She waved her arms like an air traffic controller on five Red Bulls. "Get up. Right now. You can't do this. It isn't the right time."

He blinked at her as if seeing clearly would help him comprehend why this woman was interfering with his proposal. "I don't understand."

She grabbed the ring box. "Oh my, that's beautiful." But she shook her head and snapped it shut. "I'll explain later. I know Kat wants to marry you. Trust me, though, put that away and don't pull it out today."

Wes stood and stared down at the crimson-colored box.

Behind her, Kat walked arm in arm with her other two friends he recognized as Tracie Latimer and Wendy Lively, or Trace and Wind.

Jewels handed the ring back to him and pointed to his pocket. "Put that thing away for now. Please. Just trust me. Don't ask her right now. You'll understand later."

He wasn't a man used to taking directions from someone else, but in this case, he had to yield to the advice of Kat's lifelong best friend. At the sight of Kat's pale skin and downcast gaze, disappointment turned to concern. "Is she okay?"

"I'm fine." Kat pointed to each of her friends. "Trace, Wind, Jewels, meet Wes. Wes, meet the girls."

Wind curtsied. "Charmed, I'm sure."

Trace flipped her blonde hair from her face and glanced up at him. "Ignore her. She's not housebroken. Kat's going to be okay. Just a touch of a stomach bug. We had her resting at our place."

He'd always been good at reading people. That's what made him great at running a company and building it to where it was when he sold it, and his gift told him something more was happening here. The way that Wind's gaze darted about and she hopped around like a jumping bean told him something was off. "Flu?" he asked, giving them a chance to say more.

Jewels unlocked the front door. Apparently, she had a key to Kat's place. *He* didn't have a key.

He shook off his suspicion and focused on Kat. "Hi, love. I'm sorry you're sick."

Kat straightened and released her friends for a chaste kiss to his cheek.

Not what he'd imagined, but he had to accept it without complaint in front of her gaggle of girlfriends. He knew how important their approval would be if he wanted a happy wife. "Can I get you anything?"

"No, I just need to lie down for a bit. You should stay away from me so you don't get sick," Kat said, as if urging him to leave instead of welcoming him with open arms. Something more was up here, he could feel it. But he wasn't a man to leave a situation because it was uncomfortable.

"I think I'll be staying and taking care of you." Wes swooped in, lifted her into his arms, and carried her over the threshold. "Bedroom that way, I assume?"

The grand entry was framed by a massive spiral staircase along the far wall that ascended twenty-plus feet. A mahogany railing with iron spindles accented the conversation piece.

Wind ran to the stairs and pointed up to the landing. "Oh, my goodness. It's like when Rhett carried Scarlet in *Gone with the Wind*."

Kat eyed her. "That would be my overly dramatic actress friend."

"I figured that out already." He offered a smile, but she didn't return it. The lower level of the house, with marble floors and crystal chandelier, wasn't anything compared to the crown molding and Oriental rugs on the second story.

She pointed to a room ahead. The long, wide hallway

gave way to double doors leading into a massive master bedroom. A four-poster bed was arranged between bay windows with an ocean view a few blocks away and a fireplace. Who needed a fireplace in Florida?

Kat had been right about one thing... The house was large but sterile. It was a show of wealth, not a loving home. She'd never invited him to meet her parents and he'd never been to Summer Island because she said that was her past and he was her future. Why did Kat buy this place? One of the many questions he wanted answered as soon as she felt better.

Wind yanked down the covers, and he placed Kat on the bed, then covered her with a blanket in the cold, white room. There were small dark circles framing her eyes, and her cheeks were hollow as if she'd lost weight in the few weeks since he'd seen her. Worry strangled him. "Should I take you to a doctor?"

"No," Kat said, bolting upright.

"Relax." He nudged her shoulders to the pillow, and her dark lashes fluttered open and closed.

"Sorry, you're right. I'm exhausted," Kat mumbled, but she'd barely finished before her eyes shut and didn't open again.

He studied her, the beautiful goddess of a woman who never cracked under pressure or missed a day of work. The sight of her weakened frightened him. He'd always thought of Kat as invincible. The one woman who could survive him, unlike his own mother.

"I can look after her," Wind said, her gaze darting to the other two hovering nearby.

No way he was leaving her side. If he had his way, she'd be with a team of doctors right now, but despite his need to care for her, he didn't want to overreact. Kat had warned him early on she didn't like men to hover and smother her, and he'd respected her wishes. He waved the three friends out of the room to the landing, taking a moment to tame his concern. These ladies were important to Kat; therefore, they were important to him. "It's a pleasure to meet each of you, although I wish it were under different circumstances."

"She'll be fine. Don't worry." Jewels patted his arm as if to placate his emotions that, until now, he'd thought he'd concealed well.

"I know you're all hiding something. What's going on?" Wes said in his business tone that usually had men spouting all their secrets. But inside he trembled, his thoughts tumbling into the pit of fear. "Is it serious?" His mind spun with unwanted worries. "Cancer?"

"No. Seriously, it's nothing like that." Wind fluttered a dismissive hand at him.

A coldness seeped into his soul. "So, it is something. What is it?"

Jewels grabbed Wind's arm and nudged her away. "Seriously, there's nothing wrong. She just needs some rest. I'm sure she'll feel better soon. You should chat with her tomorrow."

The way she captured his gaze told him she was telling

the truth. Part of him relaxed, but he still caught on to something. A secret among friends he wasn't privy to.

He wanted to be alone with Kat, to care for her, but they stood as a three-woman defense. With a quick glance over his shoulder, he decided to press a little further into the girl gossip. "You promise it isn't serious? You were quick to usher her in here without a word. You're not hiding something from me? I have a right to know. We might not be married yet, but we've been dating on and off for over ten years. I'm her future."

"Not hiding anything," Trace said in a business tone. "We just didn't want the epic proposal to end with her vomiting on your shoes."

If she'd seen him down on one knee, then so had Kat, unless she'd been too sick to notice. "If you're not keeping anything from me, then if you don't mind, I'd like to tend to the woman I'll be marrying someday soon."

"Can you have her call us when she wakes?" Jewels asked, backstepping away from him with the other two in tow.

"Sure."

"We'll bring breakfast tomorrow so we can all get to know each other better. Kat's important to all of us, so we all want to be there for her," Trace added before they turned like synchronized swimmers and bolted down the stairs.

She was the protective one, Jewels the motherly one, and Wind the fun and energetic one. Apparently, opposites did attract. Then how had two workaholic, power-hungry professionals ended up together?

Wes returned to Kat and climbed up on the bed by her side. She looked frail compared to the last time he'd seen her. If she wasn't better by the morning, he'd make her see a doctor. Whatever was wrong, he'd fix it.

Chapter Four

KAT WOKE sometime in the early morning hours. She rolled over and found Wes next to her, his neck kinked to one side, shoes still on his feet. The man was a vision. They'd make a beautiful and smart baby together.

No.

That's not what either of them wanted. She'd prayed not to be pregnant. She should've gone to the store with the girls to discover the truth instead of worrying over nothing. If it was a stomach bug, she'd be able to shake it off in a few days and they could jet away together.

He'd had news to tell her, and she longed to talk to him about their future plans full of travel and sun and love. She wanted to hear anything to distract her from the worry. The worry that she'd lose the most perfect man in her life. Wes wasn't the fatherly type. He'd expressed on more than one occasion that he never wanted to have children.

She would never put her child through what she'd

been through. Her child would never feel unloved or unwanted and would not be raised with parents in a loveless marriage. If she was pregnant, she'd be there for the baby no matter what. She'd never miss a dance recital or softball game or a second of making memories.

With the nausea fading, she slipped from bed, untied his shoes, and slid them from his feet. Poor Wes would wake up with a neck and back ache if he didn't get comfortable. He had taken care of himself and looked thirty-five instead of fifty-two. A full head of dark hair with a dusting of oh-so-dashing gray. Tall and lean but strong, not just of body but of mind. The connection she felt for him she'd thought impossible for a woman with no heart. How could she have a heart when she'd been taught how to never show her feelings or let them get in the way of her accomplishments? It was the Stein way.

He'd chipped away at her exterior shield over the years and found his way to her heart. She trusted him, respected him, loved him. She pressed a kiss to her sleeping handsome prince and prayed this was only a ripple in their future plans.

His eyes shot open, and he bolted up, knocking his skull into her mouth.

"Ouch!" She jumped away, holding her lips.

"I'm sorry. You scared me." Wes was at her side before she could even reach the mirror to check for blood. Not that she could see in the dim moonlight shining through the window.

"Let me see." He guided her over to the nightstand, picked up his phone, and shined the light on her face.

"Looks okay." He turned off the light, dropped his phone on the nightstand, and cupped her face. "I'm so sorry. I'd never hurt you." He kissed where he'd bumped her face with gentle sweeps of his lips, sending a flash of heat through her body.

She longed for the connection with him, but she couldn't accept his attention. Not until she knew for sure if she'd end their future with an unwanted surprise. She took a step away, but he didn't let her go. He leaned in for a real kiss, so she turned her head away. "Don't. My breath."

"I don't care."

She covered her mouth. "You will."

He nudged her hand out of the way and claimed her lips. A deep, heart-pounding, I-can't-be-away-from-you-another-second kiss. She lost herself and her thoughts if only for a time. He was her medicine for everything in life. The man she could count on to be by her side and never let her down.

Until now.

He'd accepted everything about her from day one, but he'd never accept a baby.

She broke the kiss but wrapped her arms around him and held him tight, hoping she'd never have to let him go.

"How you feeling?"

"I'm okay." She yawned. Her body still felt like it had a fifty-pound weight strapped to every muscle.

"You need more rest. Come." He tucked her into bed and then headed for the door.

"Wait. I want to stay up and be with you. I missed you."

He climbed in next to her. "I won't leave your side tonight or any other night from now on."

She knew she needed to tell him the truth, but she needed to know what that was first. Tomorrow, she'd figure it out, and then she'd know if she'd be telling him yes to marriage or no to their future together.

When tomorrow came, she woke with his arms wrapped tightly around her in a protective way, snuggling her into him as if he'd die if he didn't feel her close. She snuggled down into his embrace, and he kissed her head.

Bliss.

Until it wasn't.

A rapid boil roiled up from her belly and surged into her throat. She threw the covers off and raced for the bathroom, landing on her knees hard.

He was by her side, kneeling, holding her hair. "I'm here."

Mortified, she pushed at him to leave, but he didn't budge.

"I'm not going anywhere."

When her stomach stopped churning and she could finally breathe, her inner voice whispered, *Your body doesn't even want the baby. You're too old.*

Wes lifted her from the cold tile and set her on the bench near the tub. He grabbed a washcloth, wet it, and knelt in front of her, dabbing at her face. "My sweet girl. Is there anything I can do to help?"

A few tears slid from her eyes down her cheeks. Mortified, she covered her face, but he didn't ask or pry or demand to know why she cried; he only pulled her into his arms and held her tight. "Shh. I'm here, and I'm not going anywhere."

She needed to tell him now before he asked her to marry him and she had to tell him no again. She couldn't hurt him like that. She grabbed the rag from him, wiped her face clean of tears, and faced him.

He sat back on his heels, his hands resting on her thighs. "What is it? You can tell me anything."

She opened her mouth, but she couldn't speak. *Tell him. Tell him now.* "I might..."

Her stomach revolted again, and she ran for the toilet. This time, she shut the door to the toilet room. Why was this happening to her? She'd done everything right. The doctor should've warned her if the pill wasn't going to be as effective. No, it was a virus. A nine-month kind.

The doorbell rang, so she flushed, stood on shaking legs, opened the door, and faced Wes with the sweetest smile she could.

Stomach bug. That's all. "Would you mind letting the girls in? If not, they might break through a window to make sure I'm okay."

His face went from tight and expectant to lax and defeated. "Sure. If that's what you want." He turned on his heels and left the bathroom. Guilt wormed its way into her belly, but there was no room in there for it since something else might have taken up residence.

She washed her face, brushed her teeth, and made her way downstairs, where she spotted Wes hovering near the girls in the massive chef's kitchen, speaking in a commanding tone that would make most people squirm.

"I want to know what's going on. What's making Kat so sick? You told me it's not cancer."

Dear Lord, that's what he thought? She wanted to run to him, hug him, and tell him there was nothing to worry about. But she'd be lying, so she plastered on a happy face. "Hi, ladies. Wow, it looks like it's going to be a beautiful day."

Thank goodness they'd brought bagels and cream cheese instead of something that would stink up her house and haunt her for the rest of the morning. She felt like she was back in college.

"You're looking better." Wind flew to her side, but her gaze traveled from Kat's disheveled hair to her pale skin to her frumpy robe. "Well, mostly."

Kat smacked her and went to Wes. "See? I'm already feeling better. I think I'll eat."

"Great." Jewels unpacked a bagel, cut it in half, and put it on a plate for her. "Why don't we take it upstairs to the rooftop? I'm sure the morning air will make you feel even better."

"I'll make some coffee." Trace went to the kitchen, leaving Wes to look at her with an accusatory gaze.

"We can talk later, I guess." Wes's irritation wasn't hidden by his faux smile and sweet kiss to her cheek.

Wind slid her hand into the crook of Wes's elbow and led him to the stairs. "Come with me. I need to get to know the man who captured the attention of the impossibly picky Kat."

Jewels hung back with Kat. "I see you haven't told him yet."

"Nothing to tell. I don't know anything, and I can't get to the store right now."

Trace ran past them. "I'm on it. Look under your bathroom sink later. We brought the test for you."

"Thanks," she managed to squeak out, but she didn't really *want* the test because if she took it and discovered she was pregnant, she'd have to tell Wes. And then Wes would be gone, or worse, he'd stay out of obligation and resent her the rest of their days.

She wouldn't let that happen. If there was one thing she swore she'd never become, it was her bitter mother.

Chapter Five

Wes set into Wind the minute they reached the stairs. "So, what's really going on?"

"Whatever do you mean?" She kept hold of his arm, but her expression, staged to look like shock, didn't pass the screen test.

"You ladies are keeping something from me about Kat. Jewels stopped me from proposing, and then you swooped in and rushed me away from Kat this morning. Not to mention she's been so ill she can barely stand up."

They reached the top of the spiral staircase to the roof. The view stretched for miles, and from this spot, he couldn't tell where the river ended and the ocean began. He admitted this made the house worth it.

"She's fine, don't worry," Wind waved him off and faced the ocean view.

"Fine, I'll ask Kat to marry me now."

He had no intention of asking her anything now with all the drama surrounding them but hoped to nudge Wind into spilling the secret, so he went down on one knee and waited for the door leading to the house to open.

Wind rushed around him, blocking his view of the door. "She's going through something, that's all."

"What? If it's not cancer, then something worse?"

"No. I can't tell you what, but..." Wind ushered him to stand and then sit in a chair at the round dining table near the corner of the deck. "She's ill but not sick. Not really, so there's nothing for you to worry about."

"And?" He waited for more information. "I'm not into riddles."

The door flew open, and out poured the rest of the women with Kat in tow. She still looked weak and tired.

"Ill but not sick? What's that supposed to mean?" He eyed her then Kat. And then Kat's hand resting on her belly. A thousand needles pricked him at once.

No.

It couldn't be true.

He'd vowed never to get a woman pregnant. Ever. Especially not Kat. "You're pregnant?" he shouted more than asked. The shock plowed through him. Heat seared his skin like it was a sun index of 1000.

"You told him?" Trace smacked the back of Wind's head.

"No. I didn't. He guessed." Wind turned to Kat. "Please, I didn't. I swear."

Dizzy, sick to his stomach, he thought he'd pass out. The breeze didn't blow across his skin. The oxygen didn't enter his lungs. The world didn't turn yet spun around him. "I—I—"

Kat lifted her chin and waltzed up to him. "I don't know that I'm pregnant."

Her words sounded like placebos to cure a brain tumor.

"You don't know? I thought you were on the pill?"

"I am. I don't know how it happened or if it even did." She released him. "But this isn't your concern. If I'm pregnant, you're free. I won't hold you to any obligations."

Her words came out strong, but her bottom lip trembled.

He stood there, his mind still spinning, his gaze darting from upset friend to disapproving friend to I'm-going-to-lynch-you friend. Then he caught Kat's gaze, and for the first time ever, he saw something in her eyes he thought he'd never witness: fear. It gutted him. He hated himself more than ever for risking her life like this, but in that moment, he knew one thing... He'd never abandon his responsibility or Kat.

He grabbed her hand and tugged her to him. Ignoring his pulse-thumping fear of losing her, he had to be the rock she could lean on. "I'm sorry. I didn't handle the news well. It's a shock, that's all. I don't know what to say or what to do at this moment. But there's one promise I *can* make. I won't leave you. We'll figure this out together."

"But you don't want children." Kat tried to pull away, but he only held her tighter, willing her never to leave this world because of him.

"I said I never wanted to get you pregnant. You've said from day one you didn't want a baby. And I figured I didn't need a child if I had you."

"Aw," Wind said, reminding him they had an audience. He couldn't process this, not now. Now he had to be here for Kat.

"This is why I wanted to be the one to tell you." She shot an angry look to Wind.

"Why didn't you?" His voice ticked up to anger, despite his will to remain calm.

"Because there was nothing to tell. I don't know if I'm pregnant." Kat shrugged. "I didn't have a chance to take a test. I came home and—"

"And I was down on one knee." He realized Jewels really had saved him from an epic mistake. A proposal at that moment would've been a disaster.

"Yes," Kat said in a tortured voice that broke his heart.

Wes wanted to run far away from this, but the problem was that he only wanted to run to a deserted island with Kat. The woman he loved and never wanted to let go of. He had to know for sure if he'd put Kat in danger. If he could lose her.

No. This wasn't happening. She wasn't pregnant. He should've had the vasectomy like he'd planned, but the doctor had refused when he was thirty, and he'd never had time to return once his company grew. And over the years he'd assumed God was just and he couldn't have children. How stupid he'd been. He couldn't wait another second to find out if Kat was in danger, as his father had been with his mother, with fatal consequences. "Let's go take that test to find out. I'll run to the store."

"No need. There's one hidden upstairs in the bathroom for her," Trace said but backed away.

"If you ladies don't mind, I think Kat and I have a lot to talk about alone." Wes tried to keep his tone level, but this wasn't about Kat and her friends. This was about their relationship and their future and his failings.

"Kat?" Jewels asked.

He respected their bond and how they looked out for each other, but they weren't part of this equation.

"I'll call you later," Kat said. She followed them down the stairs, but he remained on the deck to collect his thoughts. He was scared to lose Kat, but he knew that with the medical advancements of today, very few women died in childbirth. After living with his bitter father all those years, he couldn't help but worry his child would take the life of his wife like he himself had taken the life of his own mother.

Now was the time to man up, not fall apart, but he was angry. Angry she hadn't told him first, angry she didn't trust him to be there for her, angry she was pregnant because it would ruin all their plans. Worse, angry because he had done this. He'd risked her life.

And that's why she hadn't told him. Because he'd been going on and on and on about how he was ready to have freedom and escape the daily life for a private island with her. All those dreams were lost, never to be memories. He inhaled a lungful of ocean air and clung to its calming nature.

Father.

That was a term he'd never allowed himself to consider. He'd made sure he had no time for family. Heck, he probably wouldn't have done anything but work and jet-set around the world if it hadn't been for the fact that he'd met Kat. A woman like no other he'd experienced anywhere in the world. He'd dated the daughter of a sheik, a lady from England, a firefighter, a newscaster. None, not one of them, made him feel like he'd climb a mountain, swim an ocean, or jump out of a perfectly good plane to catch them.

Only Kat made him feel that way. And now she could give him something he never thought he wanted. A baby.

How would their relationship thrive with a baby thwarting their time together? His thoughts raced through all the reasons he should never want a child, from fear to loss of freedom to their age.

"I know it's a lot to take in." Kat's words came soft and wounded, catching his attention. He wanted to be there for her, take care of her, but he also wanted to run to the closest bar and have a good, stiff drink. Something he'd sworn off years ago. He stood on the other side of the table, feeling the unwanted distance between them.

"Listen, we don't even know that there's anything to

figure out here. Let's go take that test, and then we can discuss options."

"Options? I won't—"

"No. I'm not asking you to do that. Your body, your choice, but I'd never want that. All I want is for us to figure out how to face this together." Wes took her hand and kissed her forehead gently to let her know he was here by her side. *Dear God, don't let this be true.* "How late are you?"

"About three weeks. I hadn't even realized it until we were talking yesterday."

He rested his forehead against hers, wishing she would've felt comfortable enough to tell him then so they could be in the same place now instead of him in shock and unable to think. "That's what riled you up."

Kat nodded. "I know you should've been the first one I told about my suspicions, but I couldn't tell you like that. Not over video chat. And then yesterday when I tried to go see the girls, I couldn't keep anything down and they guessed. We were on our way to get a test when I received your text that you took an earlier flight, so we came here. I only wanted to be with you, spend time with you, and I convinced myself it couldn't be true."

Wes wanted to say a thousand things to Kat—they were too old, they had plans, they wouldn't be good parents, that she could die in childbirth—but he couldn't say any of those things. He guessed she'd probably thought of all the reasons they shouldn't have a baby already, but here they were. So, all he could say was, "Let's go find out."

He took her by the hand and concentrated on staying upright, shuffling forward step by step, and breathing.

His lungs seized, his heart pounded, his stomach churned, and he wanted to run away. But he stayed because Kat needed him. And he couldn't live without her.

Chapter Six

Kat sat on the corner of the bed by Wes's side, waiting the allotted amount of time for the stick to tell her if she was pregnant or not. He'd handled it better than she'd given him credit for, because he was still here. If she could run away from this, would she have stayed?

A baby was a blessing, but not for them. They'd be using walkers by the time the kid reached college.

"Whatever the answer, we'll handle this together," Wes said, but she'd been an attorney long enough to know when someone held back the truth. And the truth was, he was as frightened as she was to face this.

The timer on her phone sounded, so she shut it off but didn't move.

"You want me to go check?" Wes offered, the same way he always offered to handle everything, but she had never needed a man to save her. She wasn't going to start now.

"No." She turned sideways to face him. "This could

change everything between us, and I want you to listen to me."

"I'm not—"

"Leaving, yes, I know. You're saying the right things and doing the right things, but I can see that you're struggling as much as I am. I want you to know that the door's open and I won't resent you for leaving through it. You have plans, big plans, and this could take them from you. I know I've pushed you away and thought I never wanted to get married and that I never wanted kids, but here we are. You're not tied to me legally. You can go."

"I should've known. Only a lawyer would think of it in legal terms," Wes teased, but he did that when he was nervous. "Give me a chance here. I need to catch up to where you're at. I just found out, so I'm still processing."

Kat wanted to fall into his arms and get lost in his love forever, but it wasn't an option to do that anymore.

"I'm staying, so go look at that test before I do." Wes's leg shook with nervous energy the way her insides shook with fear.

"Fine, but once we look, there's no going back. We can't deny the truth, whatever that may be."

"I was a lawyer too, so we can argue the legalities of custody and marriage later. But for now, let's figure out what we're facing." Wes pointed to the door. "Now go."

Kat walked into the bathroom and remembered how Wes had held her hair as she was sick, the tender touch when he dabbed at her face with a cloth, the soft kisses and concerned looks. He was a good man. And if she ever wanted to have a baby, it would be with Wes. But she didn't, so she closed her eyes and lifted the stick, willing it to be negative.

After three deep breaths, she knew Wes was right. Not knowing was worse than facing it, so she opened her eyes to see, but there were no lines in the result window. It wasn't positive or negative. "What?" she shrieked.

Wes flew into the bathroom and took her into his arms. "It'll be okay. We'll figure this out."

"I'm not pregnant."

He slid from her arms with the biggest smile on his face, the relief flooding color back into his skin. "What a relief."

"I mean...I don't know. The darn test shows inconclusive." Kat threw it into the sink and paced the floor. "This is ridiculous. Maybe I've hit menopause. Lord knows I'm old enough. Okay, maybe a little young for it, but some of my friends have hit it in their late forties and early fifties."

Wes retrieved the darn stick and analyzed it like her Harvard law degree didn't equip her to read a home pregnancy test. "It's inconclusive."

"Why don't men believe a woman when she says something? They always have to check the results for themselves." Kat rubbed her aching forehead. "Sorry. I'm tired, and I'm queasy, and I'm confused."

Wes guided her back to the bed. "Lie down and get some rest. I'll go get another pregnancy test, and we can try again."

"No, I'll make an appointment to see Jewels's ob-gyn.

I'm not going through this again." Kat grabbed her phone and texted Jewels for the number. *This wasn't happening. It couldn't be happening.*

Once she went back and forth with Jewels, explaining the results, she finally sent the number. Why did everyone question her ability to read a darn stick with lines? She called the doctor's office and spoke to the receptionist.

"She has a new patient appointment in six weeks."

"Six weeks?" Kat shrilled, forgetting all her courtroom training. "I'm a fifty-year-old woman who hasn't been able to keep anything down for over a week. I can barely stand up, and my head is killing me."

"Hold please."

Kat held the phone away from her ear. "Elevator music, really? I might have to reach through this phone and make my own appointment."

Wes looked at her with a crooked smile.

"What?"

"I forgot how breathtaking you can be. You know I used to slip into the courtroom to watch you during a trial?"

"You did?"

"Yep. The first time I saw you argue a case, I knew I loved you. You're the most powerful woman I've ever known."

"I miss her." Kat sighed. "I don't like feeling weak."

"Hello, Ms. Stein. Dr. Ryland can see you at two p.m."

"Thank you." After giving insurance information and answering a bazillion questions, Kat finally hung up the phone and fell back, her eyes barely able to remain open. "I need to take a nap. Make sure I'm awake by noon."

Wes tucked the covers up to her chin. "Don't worry. Just rest. I've got you."

She was in and out of sleep and heard him pacing the hallway and looking in on her every five minutes, but she didn't have the energy to speak to him. If she wasn't pregnant, something really had to be wrong. She covered her stomach with her hand, and a strange sensation came over her, a warmth from deep inside, a connection she couldn't explain. At that moment, she knew that if she was pregnant, she would do everything to be a better mother than her own. No nannies, no caregivers—she'd raise the baby without a nanny or Wes. She was strong. Strong enough to be a single mother. She'd won impossible cases against the top lawyers in the nation. How hard could single parenthood be?

Chapter Seven

WES PACED the doctor's waiting room. The office was in an old cottage and felt more like a home than an office. Thankfully, it smelled of flowers and perfume instead of disinfectant and alcohol.

Fancy drapes hung around the windows with tassels dancing each time the old air conditioner rattled, sputtered, and cut on, shooting cooling air onto his heated skin.

He should be back there holding Kat's hand, not stuck out here, helpless.

The receptionist cleared her throat and pointed to a chair next to the large fish tank. Why did doctors' offices always have fish tanks?

The gurgling irritated him. The light shining in between the wood slat blinds across the room irritated him. The woman clearing her throat at the end of the row of uncomfortable chairs irritated him.

How had they gotten here? They'd both worked too

hard to earn their financial freedom to face the shackles of children. Perhaps if he'd been around children or he had fatherly instinct, he'd be happy about this, but he lacked any parental skills. He was never meant to be a parent.

He wasn't sure if he worried more about if there was a baby or if there was something more seriously wrong with Kat. At the moment, he wished he had his own Friendsters to lean on. A group of men by his side, telling him everything would be okay, that Kat would be okay.

A nurse in bright pink scrubs opened a door and stepped into the waiting room. "Mr. Stein, you may come back now."

Irritation poked at him again, but he rose without correcting the woman about his last name. Dots exploded in his vision, but he managed to blink through the gray and make out the path to the innards of the doctor's office.

Stress took a toll on everyone. He'd always managed well throughout his career by going for a good run, but he hadn't wanted to leave Kat for even five minutes. Not when she was sick over and over again. Poor thing. He wanted to make this better for her. He wanted to make this right.

At the end of the hall, they hung a right and the nurse pointed into a large office, but Kat wasn't there. His heart skipped and skidded to a stop. "Where's Kat?"

"Stay calm, Mr. Stein. She'll be here in a few moments. She's just getting dressed."

No. He'd fix this, especially if Kat was caring his child. She'd have his last name by the end of the day. If Kat didn't agree to let him put a ring on her soon, he'd go insane. She was his responsibility, and he needed to take care of her.

A mist spurted out orange and lavender scents from a contraption in the corner. Why would they put something like that in an office with pregnant women? According to Kat, every smell made her sick.

Stay calm. Take a breath. He repeated this mantra over and over and over again to himself. He couldn't fall apart when Kat needed him.

She entered the room, her face pale, hands shaking, and wearing a forced smile. "Hey, there."

He reached her side but was scared to touch her, as if he'd break her with one finger. "How you doing?"

"We'll know in a few minutes. As you wished, I waited to know anything until you were by my side."

He touched his forehead to hers and held both her hands gently. *God, please don't let her be pregnant. Don't take her from me.* "We'll get through this together."

"Thank you for being here with me," she whispered.

"Did you ever doubt me?"

"I doubted myself. I'd be gone if I were you." She chuckled, but he knew she had the strength of a hundred men and would never have run off.

A woman with a white coat entered the office from a door at the back. She placed a tablet on the desktop, then offered her hand to Wes. "Nice to meet you. I'm Doctor Ryland."

He reluctantly released Kat's hand. "Nice to meet you."

She had a firm, business-like handshake he respected.

"Please, sit." Dr. Ryland pulled a chair around near them instead of remaining on the other side of the desk. This couldn't be good.

Wes pulled out a chair for Kat and held her elbow until she was safely in the seat, out of fear she'd collapse at any moment. He wouldn't let her fall, ever.

Dr. Ryland smiled at them both, a warm yet alarming I've-got-bad-news kind of soft-eyed look. Wes's stomach bubbled faster than that darn fish tank had gurgled.

The room spun with ensuing panic. *Don't let her be pregnant.* Kat. That's all he cared about. "Is she okay?"

"Please, take a breath, both of you. I know you've been stressed, and that hasn't helped Kat at all. After reviewing Kat's medical records, speaking with her, and completing her examination and urinalysis, I can tell you that you're indeed pregnant."

Wes fought to remain seated. Energy flooded through him, and he thought he could run an ultra-marathon and beat the twenty-year-olds.

"Run. Run now. I would," Kat said in a joking tone, but he knew it was a real offer.

"Told you, I'm not going anywhere." He managed the words, even if they were shaky. He lifted her hand to his lips and kissed her knuckles.

"How did this happen?" Tears pooled in her eyes. "I'm on the pill. Not to mention my age. How does a fifty-year-old woman get pregnant?"

"It happens. We may not ever know for sure, but I have a theory about why your oral contraception failed."

"How?" Kat asked.

"You've been taking dietary supplements. One of them has St. John's wort in it, which could interfere with the oral contraceptive. That being said, we will never know for sure."

"God's will," Kat murmured.

Wes snarled at the textured ceiling. "God's will for people our age to get pregnant? He does know this isn't the ancient times where people lived to be hundreds of years old, right?"

Kat squeezed his hand as if to be the one calming him.

"I understand your shock. You both need to discuss what you want to do moving forward, but first I want to make sure you have all the facts and know what to expect with this pregnancy. To understand the risks—"

"Risks?" Wes asked, his blood pumping like a fuel injector.

Kat nodded. "My age."

"Yes, that's one factor. The increase of things like Down Syndrome or other chromosomal abnormalities or birth defects is a risk, but there are children born every day to women your age with no issues at all. It's a statistical increase but not a guarantee. We'll need to run some tests at different stages of your pregnancy. You could have a healthy baby. But there are other concerns at the moment. You have hyperemesis gravidarum, which simply means severe morning sickness."

"Can that harm the baby?" A tear slipped down Kat's cheek.

He swiped it away the way he wanted to swipe all her worries away. "Or Kat?"

"We'll need to treat both mother and baby with IV fluids and then start you on bland foods. I'll give you all the information you'll need on proper diet. As for the IV fluids, there's a mobile service you can call so that a nurse will come administer the treatment at your home instead of at the hospital. I believe this will decrease stress, which is the most important thing right now for mother and baby."

"Thank you, doctor." Kat lifted her chin as if taking all of this head-on would be easy.

"The reason stress is so important to avoid is due to your elevated blood pressure. However, this isn't a surprise, considering all your body is going through. I'd like you to rest as much as possible and stay off your feet the next few weeks."

Kat put her free hand to her belly. "You think I'll lose the baby, don't you?"

"You asked me to be honest, so I will be throughout this process. Yes, there is an increased risk of you losing the baby due to this being early in the pregnancy and your age."

Losing the baby? What about Kat? "Is it safer for her to lose the baby now as opposed to later?" His words slipped out, and based on the doctor's and patient's expressions, he'd been too direct. "What I mean to say is do I need to be concerned about the risks being greater now or later?" He knew he still hadn't expressed his thoughts well but shut his mouth.

"Katherine is healthier than most of the twenty- and thirty-something women I see. I encourage you both not to make any major decisions at this moment. Go home, rest, spend some time together. I'll refer you to a specialist, though. You'll be considered a high-risk pregnancy. You'll have to travel to Orlando since there are no specialists in Summer Island. I'm going to remain your physician as long as you're on the island, though. I want you to have someone close by."

He couldn't let it go. He had to know the truth. "Doctor, I still want to know more about the risks, specifically for Kat. Could this baby cause her health problems? Could I lose..." He couldn't say the words. He choked on the rising bile of terror.

"We won't let that happen. We'll keep a close eye on her blood pressure, and she'll receive the best of care. Now, I want you both to go home and rest. I'd like to encourage you to lean on those you trust, but get used to the news and give it some time before you share with too many friends and neighbors."

"Because I'm at high risk of losing the baby." Tears spilled down Kat's cheeks, and he thought he'd crumble right in front of the doctor. Never had he ever seen Kat cry like this.

Hormones. He'd heard all about them from friends and co-workers whose wives had babies. This was going to be a challenging time. He needed to be the strong one. To care for her and his unborn child.

His. Unborn. Child.

The words stuck in his mind and played on repeat.

"As I said, avoid stress and enjoy each other." She covered both their hands with hers, shocking Wes. "I'll be with you through all of the pregnancy. You're not alone. Once you get home, write out a list of questions as they come to you. You can email them to me here or call the nurse line. I check email every hour, and I'll get back to you within a short time. I'm also on call for you night or day."

"Thank you, doctor." Kat's tears slowed to a trickle.

Dr. Ryland caught his gaze and held it. "Dad, your goal is to get her to eat, even though she won't want to. The medicine should help, but her goal is to keep food down for fifteen minutes. Serve her in bed and have her try not to move after she eats. It will help her keep it down longer."

"Dad," he whispered, as if saying it too loudly would make it real.

Chapter Eight

All day, Kat fought to wake up and move around, but her body wouldn't allow it. She'd roll over, stick one foot out from under the covers, and fall back to sleep. When she'd wake again, she was covered to the neck and Wes hovered nearby.

The IV dripped into her arm, and by the time the evening sun faded, she woke long enough to see the nurse leave the room. From outside in the hallway, she heard the nurse say, "It's best to let her sleep. Try to get her to eat something when she wakes, even if it is in the middle of the night. But don't wake her."

"Is she doing any better? Should I hire a full-time nurse to monitor her health? Can I..." Wes's voice faded into the night, and for the first time in Kat's life, she couldn't find the energy to get up and fake being alright.

The morning sun speared through the darkness before the world awoke around her. Only the faint chirp in the distance was evidence of life outside the bedroom. She rubbed the sleep from her eyes and rolled over to find Wes sitting up straight in bed with his eyes closed.

She wanted to remain still to allow him to sleep, but her bladder won, and she slipped from the covers. Her toes brushed the floor.

"What's wrong? You okay? What can I get you?" Wes flew out of bed and was at her side before her heel could rest on the ground.

"I don't think you can do this for me."

"I can do anything. Just tell me what you need."

"I have to go to the bathroom."

"Oh." He stepped aside but grabbed her elbow and escorted her to the bathroom.

"I've got it from here." Kat nudged him away and stepped into the toilet room and shut the door. "I can see your shadow. I can't pee with you waiting there like that."

"I'll go if you promise to tell me when you're done. I don't want you walking without me. You collapsed last night. I won't let you fall again."

"I did?" She shook off the haze and caught hold of a vague memory of her knees hitting the tile floor. She lifted her nightgown and spotted a small bruise forming. "Okay, I promise to call for you when I'm ready."

His shadow shrunk and faded, so she took the one blissful minute to hide from the hovering husband. Okay, so he wasn't her husband, but he sure behaved like one. She needed a breath, and she took it.

When she was done, she flushed the toilet, and his

shadow reappeared. She opened the door to a disheveled, dark-circle-eyed man she barely recognized. His eyebrows angled down and his eyes narrowed. "You promised to call me."

"I didn't get a chance. You appeared the minute I flushed." Kat sighed and closed her eyes.

"What is it?" Wes took her forearm like she was a ninety-year-old crossing Main Street. "Let's get you to bed."

She wanted to snatch her arm away and tell him to stop fussing, but she saw the worry in his eyes, so she allowed him to help. Perhaps if she showed him how much better she felt, he'd give her some space.

He tucked her into bed. The doorbell rang, snagging his attention away from her, so she took the opportunity. "It might be the girls."

"No, it's a grocery delivery. It's important for you to eat a bland diet—no fatty foods, small meals, plenty of fluids when you're not too nauseated, and nutritious as possible."

"How do you know all that?" She quirked a brow at him.

"I read the literature the doctor gave us last night, and I downloaded two pregnancy books."

"I see. Go get the groceries before they spoil." She pointed to the door. Anything to get him away from her for thirty seconds so she could think.

He paused at the end of the bed. "Promise me you won't get out of bed while I'm gone."

She crossed her heart. "I promise."

He raced from the room, and she knew he'd make it back in record time. She'd only have a couple of minutes to check on work. She reached for her phone on the nightstand, but it wasn't there. She scanned the room but didn't see her cell anywhere.

Work had to be piling up, and she needed to tell the girls what was going on. When Wes returned, she noticed his wrinkled button-up shirt and pants, the stain on his collar. The man who always looked perfect appeared homeless and hopeless.

"Sit down. We need to talk."

He joined her on the bed and held her hand. "What is it? Are you in pain? Sick?"

"Please, take a breath." Kat ran her nails down his arm to soothe his worry the way she did when he stressed over some big business deal. "Listen, I feel better today. The sleep and the IV fluids helped me. I appreciate all you've done to take care of me and I love you for it, but now you need to get some rest."

"I'm fine. I slept some. Besides, I need to make you some breakfast."

"The girls can bring something over. I need to call them before they show up with the police for me being MIA this long."

"Don't worry about the girls. I already called them. They know you need your rest, so they won't be bothering you right now."

"Bothering me? They wouldn't bother me."

"Doctor's orders. No stress, remember?" Wes kissed

her cheek. "I'll go make you something to eat."

She sat up in bed. "Where's my cell phone?"

"Downstairs where it won't bother you." He returned and nudged her back to the pillow.

"I need to check in at work."

"No need. I already called, and Dave is covering for you."

She shot up. "You told him?"

"No. I mean, just that you were sick. He said take all the time you need."

Kat swung her legs over the side of the bed, ready to stand and fight, but her head spun like a merry-go-round. "I can work from bed if I have to, but I need to work. I can't dump all my clients on Dave."

Wes tucked her back into bed.

She was too weak to argue, yet she needed space and for him to let her breathe. She needed to distract him with something other than caring for her. "Wait, what about your company? I'm sure you need to head back soon. The girls can come stay with me while you're gone. I don't want to be a burden to you."

"You're never a burden. Besides, I don't need to return. I sold my company, so I have nothing better to do than to take care of you. I promised I wouldn't leave your side, and I won't."

Dear Lord in heaven, help me. Kat needed a plan. No way she'd be the project for a workaholic like Wes. She'd drown in his attention. She loved him, but she needed to love him from a distance for an hour or two.

Chapter Nine

For four days, Wes cooked, cleaned, and took care of Kat since he didn't want to hire strangers to come into her house and potentially stress her out. He couldn't remember the last time he'd taken trash out. He'd paid people to run his house while he worked all these years.

Kat slept most of the time, so he read up on all the things that could go wrong during her first trimester. He found himself checking her breathing on more than one occasion. His gut clenched tight each time she moved because he feared she'd hemorrhage or her blood pressure would skyrocket and she'd have a stroke. He'd had no idea how many things could go wrong while a woman was pregnant. So many things out of his control.

They hadn't even spoken about the baby. He didn't want to nudge her into any conversations that would upset her until they saw the specialist next week. More than once, he caught her hand on her belly, and he feared she'd grown attached to the unborn child who had little chance of making it full-term. All he could do was be there for her and support her any way he could.

He managed to make toast without burning it this morning. With toast and juice in hand and a little hint of pride for his culinary success, he tip-toed upstairs in case she'd fallen asleep again. But she hadn't. Instead, she sat up in bed with her darn cell phone in hand.

"How did you get that?" he snapped but then cleared his throat and forced a more relaxed tone. "You're doing better, so let's not cause any undue stress now, okay?"

She took the phone and shoved it into her pocket. "Enough." Her cross-examination tone rang loud and derisively.

He set the plate down on the nightstand and studied her. "What's enough?"

"You. I need some space. I'm trying so hard to be patient, but it's been almost a week. I've been able to put back on two pounds, and the nurse said I'm doing great. I can't be your job."

He sank onto the bed by her feet, his pride deflating. What was the right thing to do in this situation? How could he stay close enough to protect her but far enough for her to feel independent? How would he ever be a good father if he couldn't even be a good boyfriend? He needed to do better. She was a proud woman, and he knew this would be difficult for her. "I'm not trying to smother you."

Kat's eyes softened, and she patted the space beside her. He crawled up next to her and took her into his arms. She relaxed into his side and put her hand on his chest, making life feel normal, if only for a moment. He savored the connection between them. He'd felt cold inside since arriving in Summer Island, despite the heavy, sticky heat.

Kat ran a nail in circles on his sternum, soothing him further. "I love you, and I appreciate everything you're trying to do, but you can't manage me or this pregnancy. You're a man who's used to getting things done, controlling the situation, and so am I, but this isn't something we can control."

"I know, but we can do things to mitigate the risk." He tried to remain calm, but his heart beat against his chest as if to leap out and touch Kat's attentive hand. "You're used to being invincible, so you don't want to slow down, but you don't have a choice." His voice cracked.

She tapped his chin, coaxing him to look at her eyes, the color of burning embers. "You need to take a beat before you give yourself a heart attack." Her lips pressed to his cheek, sending warmth through him. "You've been so caught up with caring for me that we haven't talked about you selling your company. Why'd you do that? You didn't even tell me."

He brushed her beautiful, bourbon-brown hair from her perfect porcelain skin. "It was going to be a surprise. We've both been so busy for so long, and there's only so much time left in our lives that I wanted to be free for when you had some time off. Our schedules never synched. I thought if one of us didn't have so many responsibilities, we'd get to travel and spend time together the way we always talked about."

"I'm sorry." Her voice dipped to defeated. "I know I didn't do this on purpose, but I didn't mean to ruin your plans. I would've said yes." Kat cupped his cheeks and kissed his lips with such passion he almost forgot she was carrying a child.

He surrendered to her attention if only for a moment. When he found the strength to break their connection, he stroked Kat's hair and studied her beautiful nose, cheeks, mouth. He longed to see the light return to her gaze. "This situation took two of us. I don't think you could get yourself pregnant."

"You can tease all you want, but I know this has destroyed all your plans for us. I mean, you sold your company, the one you've spent your life building. Why would you do that?"

Wes pulled away and went to the window, eyeing the distant ocean. Did she still not get how much he loved her? Maybe they weren't on the same page. "I won't make you my job, I promise. When I sold my company, I planned on still working but in a more philanthropic way. I don't want to just leave a company behind someday. I want to leave a purpose."

"What kind of purpose? What kind of work?" she asked.

"Don't know, exactly." He rubbed the stiffness from the back of his neck and turned to face her. He wanted to call her out on all her refusals of his proposals and how he'd realized in that moment that she couldn't love him the way he loved her or she would've accepted him by now. But that conversation would have to wait. "We shouldn't talk about this now. I know we're in different places right now in our relationship, and that's okay."

She sat cross-legged on the bed. Her skin was no longer pale, and she appeared stronger. That was all good. "We are in the same place. We were, I thought, but I never asked you to give everything up for me."

The doorbell rang, and he didn't have to look to know it was the Friendsters. Kat had called in her team to take over. "I know. Part of me wishes you had. At least then I'd know how you felt. That I'm worth everything to you as you are to me." He marched from the room and headed to the stairs, but he didn't even make it to the second step before Jewels used her key to enter.

They were the ones Kat wanted by her side, not him. And in her condition, he had to give her what she needed, not what he wanted.

"Sorry. We didn't want to wake you or Kat if she was sleeping," Jewels offered, but he walked on past them, grabbed his running shoes, and headed for the door.

"She's upstairs. I'm sure you'll do a better job of comforting her than I have. Just try not to let her overdo it." He marched past Jewels, Wind, Trace, and all the pain. The pain of worry about Kat's health. The pain of knowing he couldn't do anything to help. The pain that he'd never make a good father. The pain that she didn't love him the way he cared for her. And he was tired of the pain.

Chapter Ten

Surrounded by her friends, Kat still felt lost and confused.

Trace and Wind collapsed at the foot of the bed, dropping old-fashioned magazines in the center, and Jewels settled by her side with a tub of ice cream and a handful of movies.

"It's like we're back in eleventh grade." Kat lifted one of the movies. "*Sixteen Candles*. You're pulling out all the cheering-up tools." She couldn't help but chuckle. "Wow, the memories."

Wind opened up the tub of ice cream, and Trace retrieved four spoons from her bag and stuck them each into the melting mint chocolate chip. To Kat's surprise, the smell made her hungry instead of making her want to run from the food. She took a small bite and savored the cool sensation on her tongue.

Trace scooped out a heap of green goodness for herself. "We'd started to worry he'd chained you to the bed."

"Might as well have." Kat stuck the spoon back in the icy goo and leaned back against the pillows Wes had fluffed twenty times.

"I know people," Trace said. The scary thing was that she probably did after her issue with the death of her assistant and what happened with the lawsuit, but she was only teasing. Probably.

"I know. You're my girl if I ever need a body hidden." Kat laughed for the first time in a week. "But no need. He's not being the problem here. It's me. I'm irritable and tired and sick, not only my stomach but sick of lying around all the time. He's been amazing. Amazingly suffocating. I mean, he follows me to the toilet and cleans my house and cooks me food and won't let me out of this bed."

"Oh, the horrors of an attentive man who cares," Wind said with a hint of bitterness.

"What's going on with you?" Kat looked to Wind, but she only lifted a spoon and shoved ice cream into her mouth.

"Not my day," she mumbled, a drip of green oozing from the corner of her mouth.

Kat lifted a magazine and flipped through it. "I know he's being amazing, but I don't know how to process all of this. I'm used to being in control of everything around me, and so is he. I don't know this man." She swatted the picture of some hot model with her palm. The smack echoed between the wide white walls. "He sold his company because he thought it would give us more time together to travel the world when I had a break from work. And now..."

"And now you feel like you've stolen that from him." Jewels nodded. "I get it. When I found out I was pregnant with Bri after high school, Joe insisted we get married, but I didn't want him to give up his life to be a father."

"But Joe would've done anything for you. He worshiped you until the day he passed. You know that." Kat saw their relationship clearly, unlike the muddy shores of her own with Wes.

"I do. And the man I saw leaving here wasn't running away from you or avoiding what's going on, but he's struggling with processing all of this as much as you are. He's scared."

"So am I. He's not the one who has to carry the baby for the next seven and a half months, and that's only if I don't miscarry."

"But he has to worry about you, and he feels helpless to make you feel better. Men want to fix everything," Trace said in the most sympathetic tone Kat had ever heard from her.

She tossed the magazine aside and fell back again, her head throbbing like it had on and off the last few days. "I hadn't thought of that. Still, he shouldn't have sold his company. He said he wants to concentrate on philanthropic work but has no plan on how to do that. I mean, I can't run away with him even if I wanted to, and that's the problem. He was ready to abandon his life's work for me, but I couldn't lie to him. I like my life. I like work. I like being around all of you."

Jewels stroked her arm. "And that's why he bolted. He was hurt."

She could only nod. "He saw the doubt in my eyes when he declared he'd give anything and everything up for me." She reached for her spoon again to drown her misery in green goo. "Maybe I'm too selfish to love anyone like that. Maybe I have too much of my parents in me."

"Hogwash." Wind shoved the magazines aside and scooted closer as if Kat couldn't hear her from the end of the bed. "You listen to me. You're nothing like your parents. You're going to make an amazing mother and an even better wife. You both need some time to process everything. Talk about how to handle things."

Kat had always appreciated Wind's counsel, especially since she was Kat's opposite in every way. "But what if I hurt him again? I'm desperate to make him happy but also not to lose myself to do it. Not to mention, I'd never want to trap him into marriage."

Jewels passed her the tub of sugary goodness. "Take it one day at a time. Don't think about next week or next month or next year. Live in the now."

"Easier said than done. I'm not you." Kat looked at her belly. The connection she felt with something pea-sized she didn't want was mysterious and scary and wonderful. "How can I face a pregnancy and a future as a mother if I could lose it tomorrow?"

They all swooped in for a Friendster hug. "We'll all be here to help you pick up the pieces."

And she knew they would. They'd always been there for her even when they'd been apart all those years. Deep down she knew she could call on any of them and they'd come running, as she would've for them. But where did that leave Wes? He wanted all her attention and all her time. That wasn't the man she'd fallen in love with. She didn't know this man. He was a workaholic with no job.

The girls put the movie in the player and settled on the bed to watch.

"You really think Wes's just in shock and needs time to process?" Kat asked, hoping to hear the answer she wanted, not the truth.

"Yes. And he needs to see you get better," Jewels said in her motherly tone.

They watched half the movie. Not that Kat comprehended five minutes of it, because she couldn't help but think about how Wes looked when he'd fled the room. She'd broken him—an unbreakable man who handled everything in a soft but unyielding way.

Kat drowned her sorrows in more ice cream and settled back, her eyes drifting shut until her stomach shimmied and shifted and stormed up her throat. Shoving Wind off the bed, she ran for the bathroom.

The ding of the front door alarm sounded, but she couldn't stop expelling the ice cream. She heard his steps up the stairs and the girls greeting him before she finally managed to recover.

Shaking, with watery eyes and an unsteady gait, she managed to return to the room, where Wes stood drenched in sweat and an angry furrowed brow.

"Ice cream?" He shook his head. "I think Kat's had enough company for one day. If you ladies don't mind..." He helped her back to bed.

The girls shuffled out her door. "Call us if you need anything," Wind said over her shoulder as Wes ushered her out the door.

"I'm sure you can see yourselves out since you saw yourselves in," he said in an unwelcoming tone.

Ouch. Kat cringed. Usually she'd scold him for speaking to her friends that way, but exhaustion and fatigue stole her words.

When he turned around, she saw what Jewels had tried to tell her. He was being torn apart by worry for her health. "I'm sorry if I hurt you," Kat said between yawns.

Wes removed the magazines and the ice cream, then tucked her in. "Later. Right now you need sleep. Can I trust you not to get out of bed long enough for me to shower?"

She rolled over, knowing she had no energy to argue. "Yes. I promise."

Chapter Eleven

Wes tossed and turned all night seeing Kat's expression when he told her about selling his company. The way she relaxed around her friends but tensed when he entered the room made him feel like a foreigner in her life.

One thing he realized was that she needed her friends, and he wouldn't take that from her, but they needed to obey the doctor's orders and not feed her junk or get her too excited. It was time for them all to sit down and chat about what was best for Kat, not themselves.

In the morning, he let in the nurse and carried the toast upstairs.

Kat opened her eyes and lifted her head. "I thought we were good and didn't need any more IV treatments?" she asked.

"You were sick last night, and the nurse is going to stay with you a couple of hours while I give you a temporary break from me."

Kat reached for him. "I'm sorry. I didn't mean to—"

"It's fine." He gave a chaste kiss to her soft cheek. After leaving instructions with Nurse Gwen, he headed downstairs and texted Jewels.

Can you, Trace, and Wind meet this morning?

He didn't have to wait long before a response popped onto his screen.

You're welcome to come to my house.

No way. He wanted neutral ground. He only knew of one place that stood out in town.

How about the place called Cassie's on Main Street?

A quick response appeared. *Not a good idea. It's the central hub of STSB. How about the beach? No ears there.*

She texted directions on where to meet, so he decided to take a walk to burn some energy and then a run after he met with them. As a peace offering, he made some coffee and took a thermos with him. It was always good to start an important meeting with a gesture of goodwill.

The sun rose a quarter up the horizon, and he realized he would make a point to watch the sunrise tomorrow. Seagulls swooped in and raced toward the ocean for their own breakfasts. He reached the small patch of beach and eyed the rippling waves surging to the sand and stealing bits of grain to deposit back into the ocean.

The air smelled just as fresh here as it had on the private island. He set the thermos by his feet, closed his eyes, and inhaled the peace. He'd never thought the sea breeze carried the same effect on the Florida coast as it did in the middle of the ocean, but it did.

Peace. Something he hadn't felt in the last week. As he stood under the warm sun, the wind sweeping through his hair, the sounds of nature provided a respite from the constant stress and fear.

"It's magical, isn't it?" Jewels approached, holding a thermos in hand. Wind and Trace exited from a line of trees beyond the hotel.

He lifted his own thermos. "I see you're schooled in negotiation tactics."

She raised her brow. "I see you've been schooled on small-town etiquette."

"Touché." He chuckled. "Thanks for meeting me here."

"Neutral ground with no way the STSB can overhear."

"What is STSB?" he asked.

"It's the Small-Town Salty Breeze Line." Wind spread out a blanket on the packed sand just out of reach of the waves. "The gossip tends to move quicker than a tornado through town. Locals like Nancy Watermore and Old Lady Francie—not to mention Cranky Mannie, who happens to be friends with Skip, the mother to our semi-arch enemy Rhonda—hang out in Cassie's. We'd never want her to catch the gossip of Kat being pregnant considering her condition at the moment."

His head spun with small-town politics. "I see I've got a lot to learn about this place if I'm to stick around."

"If?" Jewels asked.

"Don't worry. I'd never abandon Kat. I'm just not sure she wants me long-term. That's why I've asked to meet with you." He set the thermos down on the blanket, and they all settled on the oversized blue blanket.

"She doesn't want you to go," Trace blurted.

The woman didn't have much to say, but when she did, he listened. "I hope not." He thought about asking them about Kat's commitment phobia but decided not to involve them in his and Kat's relationship more than necessary.

"How do you know what she wants? *She* doesn't even know."

Jewels poured coffee into some reusable plastic mugs Trace pulled from a bag she'd brought.

He took one with a nod and a smile. "Thanks."

Wind tilted her head as if to analyze him. "You love her, and she loves you. No reason for you to leave. Love is too hard to find. Don't let it slip away."

"I've tried to hold on, maybe too tight." He took a sip of the bitter blend with a hint of caramel that promised a pick-me-up. How could he ever compete with the devout friends of her youth and this life she'd known since childhood?

Jewels poured another for Trace and for herself before she resealed the thermos. "We all love Kat and want what's best for her. She might kill us for this, but at least Trace can't bury her own body."

They chuckled.

He quirked an inquisitive brow at them. "I don't understand."

"Nothing. Inside joke." Jewels took a sip of her own coffee.

"How do I compete with this? It's been the two of us from our San Francisco days to living together in Chicago when I opened a second office. We've done everything with our business lives together. Before we came here, it was Kat and me. Now we have an insta-family. I don't know what to do to be a part of her life now and in the future. I don't fit."

"There's no competition here. We all want what's best for Kat, so we need to figure out how to work together instead of against each other." Jewels pulled a key from her pocket and handed it to him. "First of all, this belongs to you, not me. I only had it to watch the place if she had to leave town, but now she has someone better to watch over her."

Wes studied the key. "I think we should work together to come up with a plan that keeps Kat relaxed and comfortable but not feeling like she's trapped. I want you three to come over daily to hang out with her while I leave to go for a run or take care of things outside the house. This'll allow her a break from my constant concern."

Jewels nodded. "We'd like that. Thank you."

"But—"

"We will adhere to instructions the doctor gave you. No ice cream or strippers." Wind waved her arm the way she apparently did whenever she tried to be theatrical.

Trace smacked her wrist. "No stress. Only girl time to get her mind off things."

"Thank you." Wes looked out over the ocean, searching for that peace again.

"What about you?" Jewels asked him. "Do you have anyone to help you de-stress?"

He shrugged. "I have friends back in Chicago and San Francisco, but obviously not here. I've got my running, though."

"How about you meet at the dock"—she pointed to the one in front of the hotel—"at around nine in the morning. Trevor, my boyfriend, and his friend Dustin, who is Trace's boyfriend, invited you out to go sailing."

Wes looked toward the path he'd taken here as if he could see Kat. "I don't know."

"Trust us. You won't go far away, and we'll have you on speed dial if Kat needs you," Trace offered, and he knew that had to mean a lot coming from the protective friend who didn't smile much.

"I haven't been sailing in years." He eyed the small catamaran and thought about how he had felt on the ocean—when he wasn't seasick—on the occasion that a friend invited him out for a sail back in San Francisco. It would be good for him and even better for Kat if he gave her some space. "You promise that she won't get out of bed without one of you by her side?"

"We promise," they said in unison as if they'd rehearsed.

"And you won't let her eat anything except what's on the list I'll leave?"

Wind held up her hand. "We do solemnly swear on the friendship code book."

"There's a code book?" He shook his head. "Never mind. I don't want to know."

"I'll tell Trever that you'll join them in the morning. We might be biased, but we think you'll like them. They're reformed businessmen."

"Reformed?" Wes eyed the hotel behind them.

"I just mean they gave up their old businesses and found their passions."

Wes had thought about finding his passion but still struggled to find what to focus on in life. The idea intrigued him, yet his attention needed to remain back at that sterile house in that oversized bed in that room with the amazing view. He offered his hand, but his lungs gripped his heart, and he thought it wouldn't let him go until he returned to Kat's side. If he could barely leave her for an hour to go less than a half-mile, how would he ever leave her to sail the ocean tomorrow? But he had to leave her in order to give her space, and he needed to come to grips with having a child.

It didn't seem possible or real. A foreign word. Child.

His child.

Chapter Twelve

A LIGHT in the hall woke Kat, and for the first time in weeks, she wasn't nauseated. She rolled over, but Wes wasn't in bed. He'd been distant since returning from his run yesterday morning, but she didn't want to press him.

She found her cell phone by her bed, so she snagged it, but instead of checking email, she found herself looking at nursery pictures. An urge to organize and prepare the way she did for a big trial sent her down the internet rabbit hole of baby-care paraphernalia.

The images of infants, wide-eyed and cooing in delight over the latest and greatest bouncy seat or swing, didn't make her smile. It sent a shock of terror through her. Terror of losing a baby she wasn't sure she wanted.

"Good morning. You have a busy day today if you're up for it." Wes came in without her morning toast.

His entry chased the wayward thoughts away. Before

he could scold her or see the fear in her face, she set the phone to the side and forced a bright smile.

"I spoke to the doctor, and she said if you're able to leave the bed and eat, there's no reason you shouldn't be up during the day as long as you get plenty of rest and don't overdo it."

Excitement flooded her. "Really, I can get up?"

He nodded and held up her robe for her to slip her arms into the sleeves. She didn't ask twice. Careful not to wobble when she stood so he didn't panic and put her back into bed, she rose and put on her robe, securing it with a bow in front.

"Are you up for climbing the stairs?" he asked, holding his arm out to her.

She gladly took it. "Yes, I'm good."

Her legs were still a little weak, but she had the strength to make it up the spiral staircase with him behind her. She was sure he'd be ready to catch her if she fell.

"Take it one step at a time. We're not in a hurry," he suggested more than ordered. That was a definite change.

They exited to the morning air. Twinkling lights were strung across the pergola and tea candles lit the way to the table where several flameless candles twinkled. A tray of fresh fruit and toast waited with water and juice in carafes.

Proposal? Yes, that's where the switch in attitude had come from. Now that she was stable, he'd ask her. Sure, they had a lot to work out. Maybe she could allow him the freedom he wanted, to travel the world, while she remained behind with the baby. Not ideal, but then their relationship had been anything but conventional. Did she want to marry him? She didn't want to reject him. And besides, if they were going to get married, they should do it before the baby came. They needed to pick out bedding, curtains, paint colors, and so much more. She longed to get to work but forced her attention on the breakfast spread ahead. "Wow! You did all this? You're going to spoil me."

He pulled out a chair and then pushed her to the table facing the direction of the ocean. "I figured you had such a beautiful spot up here, you should enjoy it. I've been wanting to watch the sunrise, so I thought you might enjoy some fresh air with me."

"Absolutely." She reached for the carafe, but he snagged it before she could and poured her a glass of water. She sat tall and straight, nervous. Perhaps she'd accept the ring and they could have a long engagement to figure things out. It was the right thing to do considering the circumstances.

"I'm not trying to smother you, but I forgot to mention she still doesn't want you lifting anything heavy or working until we see the specialist. I'm sorry. It isn't my choice to keep you confined."

She wrapped her fingers around his before he could release the glass. "I know I haven't said it, but thank you for taking such good care of me." She wanted to show him how much she cared for him. That she hadn't meant to push him away.

He gave a curt nod and retreated from her touch. She longed to tell him how much she loved him and that she'd marry him right here, right now, if he'd have her, but something held her back. Was she ready to get married out of some sort of motherly need to give her baby a father, or did she really want to be a wife? Would it be different, better, than what her parents had together? "I know I've been difficult. I'm sorry. I think it's because I've been so ill and, perhaps, pregnancy hormones. I mean, this crying thing is new to me."

He chuckled. "For me, too." He sat in a chair too far away, but she didn't say anything.

She wanted to tell him again that he didn't have to stay with her and the baby, that he could go and live his life, but after he'd been with her at the first appointment, she didn't think she could face any news without him by her side. Now wasn't the time to dig into everything, though. The girls were right. They needed to spend some time together and get to know this new version of each other. That's what an engagement was about, right? "I love watching the sunrise."

"I remember. You would sneak out of bed to head to the beach when we were on the island."

"You'd follow me." She winked, heat surging to her skin.

"I miss that beach," he said with that sexy, mischievous grin of his.

Orange arched from the horizon. "Oh, here it comes." She took the opportunity to scoot her chair around and take his hand. "I feel like we're back on our island."

He squeezed. "Me, too."

They sat quietly, hand-in-hand, and watched the sun light up the sky. "It's like a new beginning," Kat said, hoping he caught her meaning.

"Yes, a new day full of possibilities. Nothing like yesterday." He kissed her cheek, and she savored the attention.

When the sun rose, she thought about returning to bed and snuggling the morning away with him, but when the sun had fully risen, he stood and announced, "You've got a busy day."

"I do?" She blinked up at him, his image ghostly with the bright sun pouring in around him.

"Yep."

"What are we doing?" Excitement pricked at her. Ideas flooded in of them walking hand-in-hand on the beach or swimming in the ocean or having a picnic. Spending time together instead of being trapped in the house with nothing but worry around them.

"Not me. You." He nudged the tray toward her. "Eat up."

She nibbled on the toast, waiting to make sure her stomach accepted the offering. After a few bites, she decided to take the anti-nausea medicine and her vitamins. "What am I doing today?"

"Something I hope is allowed in that friendship handbook of yours."

She took a sip of water and quirked a brow at him. "Friendship handbook?" The joyous memory of youthful fun peered out from the past. "Oh, I forgot about that."

"What is it, and do I need a copy to know how to navigate Jewels, Trace, and Wind?"

"No, not unless I have to worry about you trying to date the same guy as us, borrowing clothes without returning them, or not calling when you need a tub of ice cream and a shoulder to cry on."

He offered a token grin, but he still remained stiff, as if he moved too quickly he'd break her. "Nope. Guess I'm good, then."

She wanted to get him to relax, to feel something other than the stress of their situation and make him forget her snippy attitude and lack of loving words. "It was the first contract I drew up. It was in the sixth grade when Rhonda stole Wind's backpack and claimed it was hers."

"Oh, the semi-enemy I heard about from the girls. I'm sure that's a story."

"Yep. Trace wanted to take her behind the monkey bars to teach her a lesson, but instead, we all reached a pact not to speak with her for the rest of our days. It led to us drawing up a contract that stated how we would treat each other as friends and the Union of the Friendsters was born. It was non-binding of course." She noticed his flinch at the word born. Was it because he didn't want the baby or because he feared the baby wouldn't make it? Did she know how she felt yet herself? No.

She'd never wanted to be a mother, but here she was, and she didn't want to lose her child. To fail at motherhood before it began. Yet, there were a thousand reasons why she shouldn't want a baby.

"Sometimes the best agreements are not bound by law," Wes said with a gaze that stretched the oceans and mountains and distance between them.

"Wes." Kat wanted to connect with him, longed to feel his comforting arms around her, but he only stood and cleared the plates.

"Not today. Today we enjoy. Tomorrow, we face everything. We can both use the break."

She swallowed the words that hung on her tongue and forced a happy smile.

They should talk, but he was right. They needed a day to escape and live for a minute. She'd hoped they'd spend it together, reliving their time on the island. "What are you going to do while I'm having my eventful day?"

"Sailing." He walked in front of Kat to the stairs and kept glancing over his shoulder to make sure she was okay as they descended to the second floor.

"I thought you get seasick."

He set the tray down in the kitchen and pointed to his neck behind his ear. "I hit the store yesterday and snagged one of these babies."

She picked up the plate to wash it, but he covered her hand, igniting a spark of hope. They stood next to each other in the kitchen, a breath apart, and she saw his gaze travel the length of her, but he shot away with the plate tight in his grasp. "There was a woman there who I'm guessing is the head of that STSB. I think she took lessons from a military interrogator."

"Let me guess... Her name was Skip."

"Yes, that's her."

Kat tensed. The woman would tell the entire world about who Wes was and what was going on in their lives. Her pulse quickened, and her face flushed.

His arms slipped behind her, and he guided her to the kitchen chair. "Take a breath. You look like you're going to pass out. I'll get the blood pressure cuff."

The dots faded, and her breath came full into her lungs. "No, please. Just sit with me for a minute."

He lowered to the chair in front of her, his palms resting on her thighs. "I know she's Rhonda's mother because she wanted to introduce me to her. She thinks I'm a guy escaping the city life for a time. That I'm just passing through."

Emotions swirled, and without a thought of why, tears flooded her eyes.

"I promise. I didn't tell her anything." Wes cupped her face. "Darling, I know we need to keep our secret for now. I would never tell anyone what we're going through unless we were both ready."

"I know."

"Then what are the tears for?"

"I don't know." She blubbered like a teenage girl over a boy. "I hate this."

He stood and took her into his arms, gentle and kind with no judgment. "It's okay. Your hormones are going to be all over the place. But don't worry. Once the baby's born, you'll be fine. And in the meantime, I won't leave your side."

"But how will you survive with me like this? What if you get sick of the situation? You're so distant, and if you're going to leave, I'd prefer you do it now." Her unreasonable, unjustified, hormonal words flooded out.

"Shhh. I'd never leave you. I'm the one who wanted to be with you for the rest of our days. That's a vow I take seriously. I believe it says something to the effect of for better and for worse, in sickness and in health."

She sniffled and tried to regain control. "Nothing about a surprise pregnancy with an old lady who turns into a sobbing glob of uselessness who's going to get fat and ugly."

He cupped her cheeks, a fire flickered in his gaze. "Kat Stein, you are many things, but you could never be ugly, and as for fat...?"

He claimed her lips with such passion, she thought her blood pressure would cause the gauge to explode. But she didn't care. His desire and need and words made her feel alive and wanted. And for those few minutes, she remembered the couple they were, and it gave her reason to believe they could be that couple again, if not even closer.

Chapter Thirteen

The sailboat teetered with the passing of a wave runner by the docks. Wes eyed the catamaran and hoped he didn't spend his time hanging over the side while the other men sailed. He enjoyed the ocean and boats, but his stomach always protested the movement.

"Permission to come aboard?" Wes remembered that little tidbit of sailor etiquette from his days living on the bay in San Francisco.

A man with shaggy, sun-bleached hair poked his head up from the engine bay. "Welcome. Yes, come aboard. I'm just checking things out. Dustin will be here in a minute with the cooler, and we'll head out."

Wes dropped the waterproof bag he'd bought yesterday onto the bench in the cockpit and offered his hand to Trevor. "Nice to meet you."

Trevor wiped his hands on a rag hanging from his torn and stained shorts. "Nice to meet you, too. I've heard a lot about you. It's good to put a face with the name."

"Don't believe everything they tell you." Wes could only imagine their concern about him.

"All good. They're a protective bunch, but once you're part of their group, there's no escaping again." Trevor closed the engine bay then stood and stretched. "Don't worry. It's a great group to be a part of. Just don't go to Friendship Beach without permission."

"Friendship Beach?"

Trevor pointed to an outcropping of mangroves and a rocky lagoon. "Over there. It's sacred land that only the girls are allowed on unless you receive a special invitation to join them."

Wes shook his head. "Seriously? There are Friendster contracts and sacred grounds?" He chuckled. "They had an interesting childhood."

"I think living in a small beachside town, you need friends to survive." A man with curly dark hair and broad shoulders marched down the dock carrying a cooler and passed it to Trevor, who secured it with a bungee cord at the back.

"Hi, I'm Dustin Hawk. Trace's other half."

They exchanged the obligatory firm man handshakes. Trevor revved the engine, and Dustin cast off the lines, tossing them to Wes.

The river was calm, but the fumes of the engine stirred his queasiness, or maybe it was remanents of the sympathetic nausea he'd been having along with Kat. He forced himself to study the horizon and sat out front watching the eclectic styles and sizes of the waterfront homes. Every few feet, another canal jetted off into the river.

He missed Kat already, but she wanted space and he needed time to think. How could he be there for her when they lost the baby? Everything he'd read indicated a high-risk pregnancy. If she did manage to get through the first trimester, then maybe there would be something to talk about, but for now, all he could do was be there for her.

Once they reached the ocean, the engine cut out, so he returned to the cockpit to help.

"You want to hoist the main?" Trevor asked.

Wes looked to the lines. "Why not? I know just enough to be dangerous, so you might want to guide me."

Trevor talked him through all the steps of sailing, from unzipping the stack pack and hooking the main halyard to the sail, to hoisting the main line and securing it with the clutch. It wasn't until the third time they tacked that Wes realized he wasn't seasick and found himself enjoying the ocean air and the busyness that sailing provided.

"You're a natural," Trevor shouted when Wes completed his first tack on his own.

"You're an excellent teacher. I heard you came here from Seattle to start this business. How do you feel about your decision?"

"Feel about it?" He tilted his hat up, scratched his head, and then lowered it once more. "My life began when I moved to Summer Island. I might have made money and been seen as a successful man, but true success I realized comes from happiness, and I've found that with Jewels."

"What about you?" He turned to Dustin, who was setting out fish trolling lines off the back of the boat.

"I concur with Trevor. Although, I had a tougher time adjusting at first, but once I did, I couldn't imagine living anywhere else in the world. Of course, Trace keeps me more challenged than the hotel does on a daily basis."

Wes thought about their words and how he longed for peace in his heart the way Trevor and Dustin appeared to have found it in their lives. The waves hit the bow of the boat, splashing over and draining through the trampolines. Only one of the new pieces of terminology he'd picked up in the last hour or so. "How did you figure out what your passion was? I mean, I know I want to start a charity or something of that nature, but I have no idea what or where or how."

Trevor maneuvered the boat around a rogue crab trap. The sails fluttered in protest, but a minute later they were back on track and the boat glided through the water on nothing but wind power.

Wes loved the feeling of sailing. The freedom of relying on Mother Nature more than an engine.

Trevor shot Dustin a sideways knowing look. "I pushed Dustin into working on the hotel, but in the end, I think he likes it."

"Yep, perfect for me. I get to meet new people while I live in a town where I know everyone." Dustin pointed. "There, that island."

Wes watched Trevor turn the helm, and without being told, Wes went to work tacking. "What's over there?"

"That's the spot where I hope to bring Trace to propose. We'll be working on a preservation project there this week. Since she's been an ocean activist since she could swim, I thought it would be a great place to ask her to marry me."

"Sounds like a good idea." Wes's heart fell to the pit of his stomach. How many times had he come up with what he thought would be the perfect proposal, only to have it thwarted or to have Kat say no?

"Jewels tells me that Kat really loves you and she wants to marry you, but she's scared because of the baby."

"I told her I wouldn't leave her."

"Yes, but she doesn't want to trap you either." Trevor shrugged. "So I've been told."

Even if she did manage to carry the baby full-term, they could hire someone to look after it while they traveled. Did their lives really have to be turned upside down because of them having a baby? Other people he knew traveled all the time despite their children. A good nanny could give them freedom.

Dustin reeled in the lines and then went on deck while Wes lowered the main. Trevor handled the helm. They made a good three-man team.

"I've heard you two have shared some amazing trips together," Dustin said while showing Wes how to secure the bridle to the anchor line.

"Yes, we have." Wes felt Trevor backing the engine until the anchor secured. "And I hope to make more."

"Sometimes you don't have to go far when you live in a place like this." Dustin patted his shoulder on the way by.

The rest of the afternoon, they fished off the beach, cooked hotdogs over a bonfire, and swam in the ocean. His memories kept slipping back to the private island and then to the rooftop deck this morning. When the sun drifted down in the sky, he itched to get back to Kat. He missed her and wanted more than anything to make new memories with her. Maybe Dustin was right and they didn't have to travel the world to live like they had on that magical island.

They could do both, live on the island with the child and then travel while the nanny watched him or her. But Wes still had no clue what he'd do if he stayed. There weren't many epic opportunities for major philanthropic work. What purpose would he have here beyond driving Kat crazy?

This was all pointless, considering they hadn't even seen the specialist. The problem was that Kat appeared to be warming to the idea of having a child, but Wes didn't connect to the possibility. How could he when the statistics were not in their favor? Besides, he'd never make a good father.

Chapter Fourteen

KAT SAT in the recliner in the living room with her feet soaking in a hot whirlpool spa tub. She closed her eyes and relaxed for the first time in forever. "I think I'll keep him."

"He's a good man." Wind sighed. "Marry him today if you can. If my man—I mean if a man did this for me, I would walk down the aisle with him. I'd race to a makeshift driftwood alter and tie him to it."

Jewels laughed. "Not what I see for your wedding, Wind. You need to be on stage or at a castle."

She shrugged. "People can change, you know."

Kat opened one eye. She wouldn't pass up the chance to bring up Wind's ex-boyfriend who'd waited decades only to reject her upon her return. "No sense in wasting Wes's spa day gift for the girls. Let's discuss Wind's love life, shall we? How's Damon Reynolds?"

"Oh no, this isn't about me." Wind held up her free

hand while the manicurist worked on her other. "This is all about you, hon." She turned to Trace. "Although, I heard today wasn't just about getting Wes and you some time apart. There was a mumbling on the phone between Trevor and Dustin last night. Something's up."

"Sounds like there might be an upcoming wedding after all," Kat teased, welcoming the conversation on anything other than her situation.

Trace huffed. "No big proposal for me. I'm more of the driftwood alter type."

"True." Kat sighed and leaned back in the chair, allowing the pedicurist to massage her foot free of cramps. She'd had a ton of them from dehydration before they started the IV treatments, but they'd improved some. Today she felt almost normal. For the moment, anyway. But in five minutes, she could be bawling on the floor.

Trace deflected the conversation back to Kat. "How 'bout you? If you said yes to Wes, what kind of wedding would you like?"

Kat kept her eyes closed, ignoring the question.

"I see her at a fancy church with hundreds of people her parents invited, with a reception at the country club," Wind said, her voice rising to front and center stage octave.

"I'm not sure. I see them eloping on a tropical island somewhere," Trace voiced.

Jewels remained silent for a moment, drawing Kat's attention enough to raise her head. "Mama bear doesn't have an opinion?"

"Nope. I know where your wedding should be, but I'll let you realize that in due time."

Kat put her foot back into the tub and lifted the other one. "You can't leave me hanging like that. If you know me so well, what do I want? I can tell you it's neither of those." In truth, she didn't have a clue.

"I'll say this. It won't be a grand event with your parents because you couldn't care less if they come or not. And you wouldn't want the attention of a thousand strangers."

"That's true." Kat shot Wind a look, but her friend stuck her tongue out like a five-year-old.

"And you wouldn't elope."

"Why's that?" Trace asked.

"Because she'd never marry without her friend family."

"Better not." Trace shot her an I'll-hunt-you-down look.

"Then where?" Kat asked, curious about Jewels's wisdom on the matter. Somehow she always knew what they'd do before it happened.

"Nope. Not going to say."

"She's lying. She doesn't have a clue, so she's making this up." Wind pouted, showing she couldn't change, but that was okay. Kat loved her the way she was. The problem was her high school sweetheart had rejected her now for being too...Wind.

"Don't you recall when Jewels told us that Rhonda would toilet paper my dad's house if we called her out in the lunchroom, and the next morning damp tissue clung to the roof and trees and we had to clean it up?" Trace grimaced at the memory. Her father never punished her, but he always taught her the value of caring for the world around her. "Or when she told us that Kat's mother would order her never to see us again because we weren't worthy, and two weeks later that's exactly what happened? Or when she told us that we'd all leave and not return to Summer Island until we were old?"

Wind shrugged. "Still think she's making it up. She said I could never change, but I'll show her."

"That's not what I said. I said you don't have to change for anyone."

"Who's she trying to change for?" Trace asked.

"This isn't about me. We're discussing Jewels making things up. She can just tell us after Kat announces where she's getting married that she knew it all along."

"Tell you what. I'll write it down when this nice lady is finished cutting my hair, and I'll put it in that vase over there. You'll all swear not to look until she decides?"

"What if we decide not to get married? What if this baby's too much? Or if I lose—" Kat choked on her words.

The woman at her feet pushed at a pressure point. "This is where you hold emotions. It will help release hormones."

After a few moments, Kat sighed and calmed down. "All I'm saying is that I'm not sure I should even marry him."

"Forever why not?" Wind pulled away from the manicurist, causing the woman to brush red polish over her hand.

"You know why. I won't make him marry me because of the baby."

"You sure that's the only reason?" Jewels asked in her motherly tone.

"What else could it be?" That he hadn't asked, or that she thought she'd lose him forever because she'd been so hormonal and mean?

The woman finished with Jewels's hair, so she stood and retrieved a paper and pen from the kitchen counter and wrote something on two pages. "First page says where you'll marry. Second one tells you why you aren't sure you want to marry him." She walked to the vase and dropped the first one inside. The second one she folded and gave to Kat. "If you want to know, you can read that. I'd advise you to wait until you're ready to face the truth, though."

Kat held the small slip of paper in her hand for a moment and decided Jewels was right. She wasn't ready to face this. "I can only think about the baby until I see the specialist. That's enough for now. Once I know if it's a viable pregnancy and there's a chance to carry full-term, then I'll face the next question, since one will affect the other."

"It doesn't have to," Trace said but then held up one hand. "But I support you no matter what. You know that, right?"

"Of course." The pedicurist dabbed Kat's feet dry and then put them on a stool to paint them. "I do have one question I want answered, though." She turned to Jewels. "When will these mood swings stop? I've cried more in the last week than I have my entire life."

"Hormones will go away once your body settles after you have the baby. As for no more tears? I'll let you know. Bri still tugs at my heart on a daily basis."

"Point taken." Kat had one last question on the tip of her tongue. "Do you guys think I'm crazy if I decide I actually want this child? I mean, I'll be old as dust by the time he or she goes to college."

"No. I think that baby is a gift you didn't know you wanted." Jewels returned to her seat. "Do you want us to go with you to the specialist tomorrow?"

Kat thought about it for a moment. She'd always turned to the girls whenever she needed anything in life, but this time she needed to face something with Wes. It was his child, too. And he'd feel left out if they went to the appointment instead of him. "No, but thank you. Wes and I will go together."

"I think that's the wise choice." Jewels offered an encouraging nod.

"Even wiser to call us immediately after, or we'll be waiting here when you get home," Trace added, and Kat knew she spoke the truth.

"If you're not too busy with Dustin down on one knee," Kat teased.

Trace didn't even look at her, but the way a smile curved her lips and her gaze danced around, Kat knew she hoped the news would be true. Trace clearly wanted to marry Dustin and start a life together.

When they were all pampered and ready for an evening out, the front door opened, and in stepped Wes, walking like a penguin. His skin, from shirt sleeve to fingertips and shorts cuff to socks, was lobster red.

Chapter Fifteen

Wes stood in the ice-cold water from the rain showerhead and appreciated the amenities of the house for the first time. His arms and legs didn't ache as much with the cooling relief, but the minute he turned off the water, the stinging returned.

He'd forgotten how much he hated sunburns.

"How you feeling?" Kat's sweet voice echoed through the oversized bathroom with vaulted ceilings.

"Like my arms and legs are on fire. Thank goodness I was wearing a hat and sun shirt. I still don't understand how I got burned. I wore sunscreen."

"Yes, but you were standing in the water fishing and on a boat and you only applied once. I apparently should've educated you before you went on your excursion." Kat held up a white container. "But I have what you need. Come and have a seat."

He sat on the bench at the far wall of the bathroom,

and Kat dipped her perfectly manicured nails into white goo, knelt by his side, and dabbed the cream onto his arm. "How was your day?"

She peered up at him through her dark eyelashes. "It was amazing. Exactly what I needed. Thank you."

Those two words sent a warmth through him. He'd done something to bring back the light in her eyes. How could he be so apt at business and casual dating, but when it came to Kat, he was challenged at every turn?

She dabbed more white product on his skin and rubbed it in, cooling relief soothing the heat. "I heard you guys went on an adventure. Something to do with either Jewels's or Trace's relationship status?"

She was on her knees at his side caring for him, not something he considered manly, yet he savored her attention. "I should be the one looking after you, not the other way around."

"Change the subject much?" She winked. Her beautiful eyes twinkled with mischief. How he'd missed that the last week.

He longed for this moment to last. "Man code. I belong to the Mansters."

She gave him her inquisitive look with both brows raised. "Mansters?"

"Yep, the male version of the Friendsters. I thought I'd have you draw up a contract for us and everything." He offered the lopsided grin that usually got him anything he wanted. Of course, from day one Kat was immune to his charms, which was probably what had gotten his attention initially. The woman could take on a courtroom and his heart without breaking a sweat.

She laughed. A light sound that made him relax and enjoy her fingers whispering over his sensitive skin. "So you're not going to tell me, are you?"

"Nope." He made like a sixth-grade girl and mimed locking his lips and tossing a key away.

She smacked his hand, sending a jolt of pain up his arm. "Oww."

"Sorry, I forgot." She brushed her lips to his fingers, knuckles, wrist, and then arm. "Better?"

His breath caught. She appeared normal. The dark circles were gone from under her eyes, and her skin was rosy instead of pale. "You're beautiful." The words tumbled from his mouth.

"You're handsome yourself, even with the farmer's tan." She moved to his leg, nudging the towel higher, revealing the top line of the sunburn. He sucked in a quick breath but steadied his desire. "Stay below the line, or I'll be having to take another cold shower."

She smiled coyly at him. Kat was many things—strong, vivacious, smart, and beautiful, but never coy. She was more the in-your-face-honest type. And he loved that about her. "Or don't."

"That's what got us into this mess in the first place, you know." He stayed her hand. "Besides, we need to see the doctor."

She nodded and returned to tending to his legs. When she closed the lid, he helped her from the ground but quickly fled from her touch and made his way to the shopping bag he hadn't even finished unloading since yesterday. He slid a Summer Island T-shirt on with a pair of shorts. "I'm sorry I ruined our dinner plans this evening."

"Don't be." Kat picked up her cell phone. "Why don't we order something and watch a movie together?"

"What about your friends?" he asked, certain she'd want to invite them over, too.

"I don't need them. I have you."

Those few words sent his heart into a rapid rise of steady beats. She needed him, was choosing him, if only for the evening.

She handed him the phone. "No matter what happens tomorrow, I want to thank you for all you've done this week."

He grimaced, remembering all the things he'd said and done wrong since hearing the news of her pregnancy. But nothing was worse than watching her struggle because he'd gotten her pregnant. Something he'd vowed never to do in his life. "I've done nothing. You're the one who's had to suffer through all of this." He brushed her hair back and kissed her lips but quickly pulled away, not wanting to forget himself. He'd done enough damage.

She snuggled into him, and he had to force himself not to flinch when she grazed his arm with her nails. "Nothing? You've gotten more than you ever thought you'd signed up for. Holding my hair as I'm sick, carrying me upstairs when I can't stand, holding me while I cry."

Would she find him weak if he confessed his truth to

her? Despite his desire for her not to be pregnant, he loved taking care of her because he felt needed by another person for the first time in his life. He'd thought he'd chosen Kat because she was so strong, but it wasn't just her strength, although she was holding up well all things considered. He dared to share his thoughts. "Is it so bad for a man to feel good when he's needed by the woman he loves?"

She looked up at him and pushed his too-long hair back from his face. "No. I think it's nice. But you don't think less of me for needing so much help?"

He wrapped his arms around her, ignoring the searing pain. "Darling, you are many things, but needy isn't one of them. That being said, no, I don't think any less of you. I think I'm more in love with you today than I was a week ago."

She blinked up at him. "But...the pregnancy and the plans."

He studied her eyes and saw that she still held back from him. As much as he didn't want her to be carrying his child, he wanted to be the man she needed even more. "You can trust me. I'm not going anywhere."

"But—"

"Let me rephrase that. I don't *want* to go anywhere. I want to be here with you. And if this child is to be, then I'll figure out how to be a father. But I don't want to get ahead of anything. Let's go tomorrow and face whatever the doctor says together. My only request is that if the doctor tells you it'll be dangerous—" he had to swallow back the emotion strangling him "to carry the baby, you'll consider the options." His voice cracked. "I can't lose you." He rested his forehead against hers. "I won't lose you." All the memories of his father's bitterness toward him for coming into this world and taking his wife in the process consumed him.

She palmed his chest. "Your heart is beating so fast."

He tried to remain calm, to not allow his past to rob him of his possible future, but his father's words were a constant reminder of what could happen to the woman he loved if she ever had a baby...*his* baby.

"It's okay. I'm not going anywhere."

He knew she hadn't really agreed to what he'd proposed. He didn't even agree with it. Like his mother, Kat would carry on with the pregnancy, ignoring anything the doctors said. All these years he'd clung to the words of his grandmother, that his father had been wrong about Wes killing his mother at birth and that his father didn't hate him. She'd told Wes that his father had only spoken through his grief. But in this moment, Wes faced his irrational fear.

He could lose Kat forever.

Chapter Sixteen

KAT EYED the tourist signs leading toward the large Mickey Mouse, but they hung a right on I-4 instead of a left. If only they were headed for happy times, not the storm that waited like the summer thunderboomer clouds rolling into shore. One glance at Wes, his hands gripped tight at the ten and two positions, and she knew he raged a war inside himself. The man didn't want a baby, but he loved her, so he would stay. But where did that leave her and the child?

She couldn't raise a child with a parent who didn't want him or her. She'd already lived that herself and wouldn't wish that upon anyone. No. Would he come around, or would she have to be the one to break things off in the end?

After all those years of avoiding marriage and commitment, determined never to become her parents, she now wanted to walk down the aisle with Wes more than anything. Pregnancy hormones? A mother's desire to give her baby a father? She didn't know, but she'd put that aside for another day.

For today, she needed him to help her get through this appointment. All her worry would be for nothing if the baby didn't make it. The thought sucker-punched her as if her unborn child let her know he or she would put up a good fight. She rubbed her belly to soothe the little dot inside her.

Wes abandoned his assault on the steering wheel and covered her hand. "You okay over there?"

"Yes, I'm fine." Kat offered a smile in hopes she'd covered the terror clawing its way to the surface. Their exit came into view, causing her pulse to quicken.

Once parked in the dim and dingy garage, he shut off the car and faced her. "I'm here with you. Let me shoulder the burden. Your job is to remain calm and know you're not alone, okay?"

She nodded, but she saw the worry etched into the distinguished lines around his eyes. "We'll go and listen to what the doctor has to say, and then we'll go from there."

Her words seemed to placate him, but when he opened her car door and took her hand, he didn't let go until they were seated in the doctor's office, waiting to speak to the person who would change their lives forever.

A man with dark, thinning hair and tired eyes entered and sat across from them behind a large wooden desk. He opened an old-fashioned folder and scanned over some notes. "Mr. and Mrs. Stein, we need to run a battery of tests to determine the health of your fetus. Due to the high-risk nature of your pregnancy, we'll need to do an amniocentesis to determine if the child has any chromosomal abnormalities, neural tube defects, or genetic disorders prior to determining whether or not to continue with the pregnancy."

Wes pulled at the unbuttoned collar around his neck. "Amnio? I've read up on that. Isn't there a risk to mother and baby?"

"There's a small increased risk of miscarriage with the procedure. We'd wait until after 14 weeks to minimize the risk. The risk factors are cramping, bleeding, leaking of amniotic fluid, infection, and preterm labor." The doctor rattled off the worst in a clipped, monotone voice.

"I thought I was already high risk for a miscarriage," Kat said, not wanting to compound the situation but needing to understand. "And I'd have to wait until after fourteen weeks?" She touched her belly and realized the dot would be a growing baby, which he'd called a fetus.

"I assure you that you'll want to determine if the fetus is viable or not. For now, let's do a sonogram and blood work to see what we can at this stage." The doctor closed the folder and walked out of the room, leaving Kat winded, her heart pounding and chest tight.

"It's okay. I'm here. Let's do the sonogram like the doctor said and then go from there." Wes squeezed her hand. "One step at a time."

The nurse guided her to another room and told Wes to wait in the lobby. He refused, and the woman stood there with mouth open. "But most husbands want to wait outside until we call them in once Mama is prepped and covered and ready for visitors."

"I'm not her husband, and I'm not leaving."

Kat flinched at the way he announced their marital status in a cold, distant tone.

Wes stood like a soldier ready to guard the queen of England.

"Mama?" Nurse looked to Kat.

"It's fine. He can face the wall if you wish, but he can stay." Kat knew she didn't have a choice if she didn't want to make a scene. She both loved and wanted to smack Wes for his overbearing, overprotective ways.

Once she was settled on the table and the woman explained the intervaginal sonogram procedures, she called Wes over and directed him to stand near Kat's head. "Now, based on your information, you should be just about eight weeks. This means we'll be able to give you an accurate due date and you can see the baby and hear his or her heartbeat."

Wes held tight to Kat's hand. She wasn't sure if he was willing the baby to be okay or wishing it wasn't there.

The nurse went to work. "Here is your fetus."

Kat really wished they'd stop calling the baby a fetus.

The woman clicked and rolled a ball and clicked again and focused on the monitor. "It appears you are just over eight weeks, so you'll be due on October 7th."

Kat swallowed a massive lump of realization. There

was really a baby inside her. She was growing a human being.

Wes leaned over her to see the monitor. "That little dot's the baby?"

"Yes." The nurse continued doing her thing. "Hmm."

"What's wrong?" Kat moved to see the monitor better.

"Stay still, please."

Wes kissed her cheek and whispered in her ear, "Everything's fine."

"It might be too early to hear the heartbeat." She moved a lever. "I'll turn it up to see if we can hear it a little."

Kat froze as if time stood still. The silence of the room a punctuation mark on whether her baby was alive. Tears welled in her eyes, but she blinked them away. The nurse moved the wand several times. The third time the nurse sighed and moved the wand, a sound broke the quiet.

Ba Bump.

Ba Bump.

Ba Bump.

The heartbeat echoed loud and strong and rapid.

Kat froze. "Should it be that fast?"

"Yes, that's normal," the nurse reassured them, but then she focused on the heart and did more things with the screen.

Kat noticed her smile at the heartbeat curve into a frown.

"What is it?" Kat asked.

"Nothing. Just doing some things the doctor requested." The nurse continued for another few minutes and then announced, "Okay, you can get dressed and return to speak with the doctor."

The nurse fled faster than Houdini after mischief. Wes faded away from her to his designated corner, and she felt the world slip from her grasp. Something wasn't right.

Something was wrong with her baby.

Chapter Seventeen

Wes usually respected a man of business, but he didn't like the doctor sitting across the table. He wasn't warm and friendly like the one in Summer Island. He realized sometimes business wasn't just business. Words he never thought he'd ever believe.

"You'll need to return in a couple weeks for another sonogram. There are some markers on the fetus that require further investigation, but it's too early for that now. We'll schedule a sonogram and the amnio, and then we'll make some decisions," the doctor said flatly.

"Wait," Kat said, her voice sounding smaller than usual. "What kind of things? Is it harmful to the baby?"

Wes had noticed Kat light up at the sound of the baby's heartbeat. He could see it made it real for her. To him, he heard the sound of a machine, but it was obvious that she'd heard life.

"Mrs. Stein, you need to understand that there is a

significant risk of losing the fetus at your age. I'd advise you to prepare yourself for the fact that this child could have cystic fibrosis, Down syndrome, or some other chromosomal abnormality."

Wes couldn't hold back his questions any longer. "Is this dangerous for Kat?"

"Mrs. Stein is in good health. Although there is always a risk, it is marginal to her, but you'll want to think about whether you'd want to raise a child with these conditions. I urge you to make a decision about termination of the pregnancy as soon as possible following the amnio."

"Terminate?" Kat's voice climbed an octave. She sniffled and cleared her throat, rose, and walked out the door with her attorney persona.

"Is there a chance that the baby will be healthy?" he dared to ask, not even sure he wanted to know the answer. This was all too much.

"Anything is possible, but it's unlikely. I urge you to look up what you'll be facing with the lifelong obligation of carrying for a disabled child."

Wes didn't offer a hand or a thank-you for his time. Instead, he hurried after Kat, catching her at the elevator headed to the garage. They didn't say a word to each other. His mind reeled and revolted with dark thoughts, but even with the worry, he clung to the doctor stating that the risks were minimal to Kat. Of course, Wes knew better.

They sat in the car, and Kat doubled over, shoulders shaking. He tugged her into his arms, longing to wrap them around her in a protective hold. That was all he could do. He felt helpless and unworthy of doing anything to make this better for her, to protect her from the pain. But all he knew was he didn't like the doctor, and to terminate a child because it had challenges didn't sit well with him. Yet, wasn't that his way out? To save Kat?

"Shhh, I've got you."

"I can't go back in there. I can't. I'm sorry. I know this isn't fair to you, but I don't care if my baby has issues. I'll deal with it. But that man, he was so cold. Like the baby was only a thing, a fetus that could be discarded without a second thought."

"I agree."

She sat straight, wiped her tears away, and looked at him with more love than he'd seen for ages. "You do?"

"I do." Boy, he wished those were words for a different reason. "But where do we go from here? I still don't want to risk you for the baby, but I don't want to give the baby up for no reason. After I heard the heartbeat..." He slid his hand over her belly, wanting to hold the little thing, to protect it like he wanted to protect Kat. "The baby became real to me. It's a real life inside you that we made."

She blubbered and swiped her eyes then threw her arms around him, holding him tight. "I love you. You're the most amazing man I've ever known."

He savored her touch and her words, but no matter how he felt, he struggled with the fear. "I need you to understand, though. If medically I need to make a choice between you and our baby, I'll choose you."

She sniffled and pulled away. "Then let's hope it doesn't come to that."

He cupped her cheek. "I hope it doesn't."

Despite the cold garage, the heat of the Florida spring forced him to release her to turn on the car. "What do we do? Do we find another specialist? I'll call around."

Kat shook her head. "No, I want to go back to Dr. Ryland for now."

He nodded. If anyone knew a better doctor, it would be the woman they'd seen back in Summer Island. He'd pay for any specialist anywhere to help. He clung to one thing the doctor had said, though. That Kat wasn't in significant danger.

Once back in Summer Island, before he could even settle in to process anything, the girls, along with Jewels's daughter Bri, Trevor, and Dustin arrived with takeout from Cassie's and Pictionary.

"You guys didn't have to come," Kat protested but opened the door wide and ushered them in.

Dustin entered, slapping Wes on the back. "How's that sunburn doing?"

"You have no room to say anything. The only reason you didn't get sunburned your first few months here was because you were scared of the ocean." Trace hip bumped him, then sauntered by with a bottle of sparkling cider.

"You're scared of the ocean?" Wes couldn't help but laugh. "Is that why you volunteered to cook instead of swimming?"

Dustin flopped down onto the couch next to Trace and

swung his arm around her shoulders. "I'm a recovered thalassophobic. Besides, someone had to do the cooking."

Trace leaned away from him as if she'd forgotten to wear her readers. "Sounds like you need some paddle-boarding lessons again."

"Nope. I'm good, but thanks."

Something told Wes there was more to the paddle-board story, but he didn't have the strength to care, so he went to the kitchen to retrieve some glasses and plates. The men crowded in to help while the women chatted in the living room.

"How you holding up?" Trevor asked.

"I'm good. Kat and I had a rough doctor's visit, but we'll get through it." Wes tried to sound convincing.

Dustin took the glasses and passed them to Trevor. "Listen, the girls have each other, so if you need to unload, we're around."

"Thanks. I appreciate some Manster time," Wes joked.

The men looked between each other then burst into laughter. "I like that. We're the Mansters," Dustin said loud and proud.

"You hear that, ladies? You might have the Friendster club, but we're the Mansters," Trevor announced to the ladies.

Wind rolled her eyes and smacked her forehead. "Great. Just what we need... A man group."

They all settled in together, eating and sipping on sparkling wine. The food from Cassie's was fresh if not a little too fried for his taste. Kat nibbled on her fish, but he could tell her stomach didn't like the flavor or the smell, so he retrieved an orange and some chicken he'd made the other night for her.

"Sorry. We should've thought about that." Jewels ushered the fish away from the group and set it on the counter. "Good thing you have Wes to take care of you."

Wes appreciated her comment and the evening. A pleasant time that gave them a chance to decompress and not talk or think about doctors and babies and what it all meant. They would have a couple of weeks to wait for the next sonogram or appointment, so they needed some distractions, and the people he'd met in Summer Island were the perfect hosts.

And for a couple of weeks, he and Kat fell into a nice rhythm. Each night he did research on different possible challenges his child could face, the limited resources for therapies, and medical care through insurance. Once he'd exhausted himself with worry and hope, he held Kat until morning, and then they'd get up and watch the sunrise from the rooftop deck while they nibbled on toast and drank juice. Nightly, they would take a walk on the beach, run errands, and have dinner with the Friendsters and Mansters hidden away in their home away from the STSB.

The morning of their appointment came with a sunrise that promised happy news, but when they left the house and reached Dr. Ryland's, Wes couldn't help but feel the swishing of concern stirring and churning his stomach.

They entered Dr. Ryland's office, and she greeted them as if she were the one excited to see them. Her smile lit up the space, and her relaxed shoulders gave him reason to feel comfortable. "I understand from Kat's emails that the specialist was too clinical and that you wish to remain under my care?"

Wes nodded, but despite his promise to go along with this, he couldn't hold back his questions. "If Kat is safe, will there need to be an amnio? If we refuse the test, will it cause any issues with keeping Kat healthy? What if—"

Dr. Ryland took him by the arm and guided him to a chair, where they all sat in a small circle together. "Let me assure you, Mr. Knox."

She'd gotten his last name correct. He sat a little taller.

"Mother's safety will be our top priority." She removed her card from a bejeweled holder and handed it to him. "I don't want only Kat to be able to send me questions. You're as much a part of this journey as she is. Please, feel free to email me anytime."

He studied the card in disbelief.

"I think you shocked him into silence. I knew I liked you. No one has ever done that." Kat's teasing tone drew him from his confusion.

"I have to agree. Not many people shock me, but you have. I'm glad we came back to you. I know Kat feels better with you as her doctor, and so do I."

Dr. Ryland sat back in her chair and folded her hands. "I need to be clear that I will still be consulting with your specialist to make sure you receive the best care possible. However, I'll be providing your treatment as long as you remain stable...which I hope to be your entire pregnancy."

"But the specialist told us we had to have the amnio and make a decision about terminating the pregnancy quick. That it would be too difficult to raise a child with a disability."

Dr. Ryland's eyes shot wide, but she quickly recovered. "As for raising a child with special needs, I can only say that it will be challenging. However, you are in a unique position that most parents are not."

"What's that?" he asked.

"Can I be blunt?"

"Yes, please," Kat said, sitting forward as if to show her complete attention.

"Money. Plain and simple, that's the difference. The care of children with unique needs can be expensive. To give them the best quality of life and future requires money for services such as therapy and specialists. Not to mention the need for respite care. Parents burn out when they don't receive breaks, and then the child suffers as much as the parents. Kat has already informed me in her emails that she'd spare no expense helping her child. That she'd hire therapists and specialists who specialize in whatever condition her child could potentially face."

"I read up on this. Most insurance companies only pay a fraction of what is needed. For instance, some children born on the autism spectrum can grow up to be independent with modern therapies, while others who don't receive these therapies end up in an institution."

Kat glanced at him with a raised brown. "Someone's been doing their homework."

Dr. Ryland offered an approving smile. "Yes. Every case and challenge is unique, but you have the ability to hire caregivers and therapists. There are limited funds for this for most families. Therefore, if you both don't want the amnio and you understand the risks of a child being born with unique needs, then I don't feel like you medically require one. That is, if it won't cause any more undue stress to mom and baby waiting to meet the baby before you know for sure."

"No, I'm fine with that." Kat sounded excited and happy. But was this really cause to be relieved?

Wes had so many more questions, but for now he wanted the doctor to run them through everything and have the sonogram done. He listened as she spoke about proper nutrition and rest, the appointment schedule, signs to look for that merited an emergency visit. The list made him squirm, but he managed to remain seated.

After a ten-minute rundown of all the concerns, she clapped her hands together and said, "Let's go meet the little one, shall we?"

She personally escorted them to a room with a lady waiting by a bed with the machine ready to go. "Hello, welcome. I'm Cindy. I'll be the one conducting your baby's first photoshoot." She smiled and patted the bed for Kat to settle on.

Wes stood by the door, waiting to be excused. "Dad, don't be shy, I'm sure you want to meet your little one, too."

Dr. Ryland waved him forward. "I'll let you two meet your baby, and then Nurse Cindy will provide some pictures for you to take and we can sit with some water or green tea and chat about what we see." She backed out and shut the door. A misting spray squirted something that smelled like mint or Eucalyptus.

Wes took Kat's hand and stood by her side, holding his breath. The lady lifted Kat's shirt a little, picked up a bottle, and shook it. "Sorry, Kat, this might be a little cold."

The nurse knew her name instead of calling her Mama. Another positive checkmark. The specialist should be here learning from this crew.

A squirt sounded, and then the wand pressed to her belly.

Ba boom. Ba boom. Ba boom. Ba boom.

"That's an excellent sound to hear. Baby has a strong heart." Nurse Cindy maneuvered the wand around, and on the screen appeared a tan creature with a head, arms, legs, and body.

"It's a baby," Wes murmured.

Kat giggled, but Nurse Cindy remained professional. "Your baby."

Wes choked up at the sight. "That little human being is inside you, and we made it."

Kat nodded. "And I don't care what they say. He or she looks perfect."

Wes tried to make out the features to see if there were any signs of any disabilities, but in that moment, he didn't care. That little blob looked perfect, and Wes's heart swelled. Swelled to a swollen ache of realization that this was real. He'd be a father.

Chapter Eighteen

THE EVENING SEA breeze brushed across Kat's face, refreshing her from the heat of the afternoon. Wes relaxed on the double outdoor daybed next to her. For the first time in weeks, he appeared relaxed, happy, excited, and it warmed her heart more than any Florida sunshine.

Kat leaned into Wes. "The girls want to throw a baby shower for us."

Wes stiffened by her side. "They'll wait a couple more weeks, right? Dr. Ryland said—"

"That in a couple weeks we are out of the major danger zone and can start to share. Relax, I feel so much better. We can choose to worry about everything we can't control, or we can have faith that it will be fine."

"Faith?" He ran a hand through his hair and let out a long breath. "Helpless is a better term. I feel this need to protect you, but I can't. Not from this." He placed his hand on her belly and held it there. It was the first sign he'd made that he'd accepted the baby, and it warmed Kat's heart. "And the need to protect this little one. This was easier before I met the little guy."

She cuddled into his side, leaning her head on his shoulder. "But you can't protect us, not from this, so just enjoy us."

He pressed his lips to the top of her head, sending a sweet comfort down her neck into her body. Things had changed between them. Sure, they'd always had passion and enjoyed each other's company, but a new connection had formed, something deeper she couldn't explain. She covered his hand with hers and could sense his mind racing. "Tell me what you're thinking."

A flash of lightning chained from the sky to the water in a jagged white pattern, stark against the darkening sky. He rested his chin on her head and rubbed his thumb back and forth on her belly, as if to soothe their unborn child. "I don't want to burden you with my fears." His voice came out rough and hollow.

She turned in his arms and faced him, capturing his soft gaze. "I'm stronger than you think, and I promise that you keeping things from me causes more stress than if you lean on me. And honestly, I won't feel like such a wimp if it isn't always you taking care of me. I want an equal partnership."

He grinned, but the lines around his eyes remained tight. "Of course you do."

Another flash of light splintered through the sky, and thunder clapped in the distance.

"We should go inside," he said.

But she wasn't going to allow him to escape so easily. "I grew up here. Trust me, we have time before that shower reaches us. We'll hear the rain coming, and the door is right there." She mustered her courage and spoke plainly. They needed everything aired out between them. "I know you didn't want this baby." She steadied herself, not wanting to get upset for the sake of the baby but needing to know where they stood as a couple. She'd avoided the truth until she heard the heartbeat and realized this wasn't about her anymore.

"It's not that I don't want the baby." He rubbed her belly and studied where the little pea-sized baby grew inside her. But then he leaned away from her, his gaze snapping to the ocean, but she guessed it was more so he could get out his words without facing her than to watch the threat approaching. "You know that my mother died giving birth to me."

Hot adrenaline shot through her. "Yes, but that won't—"

"You promised to remain calm." He gave her a sideways warning glance.

She relaxed into the pillows behind her with a nod.

"It's more than that." He cleared his throat. "I've never really told you about my father because he fell apart when I was younger. He never recovered from my mother's passing, and he never forgave me for taking her from him."

She wanted to pull him into her arms and make him see that his mother's death wasn't his fault and this was different, but the way his gaze narrowed in on the storm showed he had more to share. She covered his hand to encourage him to continue.

"When I was a teenager, he warned me that if I got a girl knocked up, I'd kill her, too. That I was a curse to all women. And even if she survived, I'd resent the child and never connect with it the way a father should. He always told me I was weaker than the mother I'd killed and that I'd never make it in this world. That's probably why I worked so hard to build an empire and avoided ever having a baby."

The truth smacked her in the face. All this time she'd thought he wanted his freedom and that's why he was distant. His fear released her from her guilt, and she wanted to do the same for him. "Wes, I'm so sorry you've lived with this your entire life." She cupped his cheek and forced him to face her. "But I'm not your mother, and you're not your father. I'm strong, and modern medicine is so much better now. I trust Dr. Ryland, and I have you. We'll do this together."

"I hated my father all these years because I didn't respect a man who fell apart from weakness. I left home at eighteen, faced a war overseas, returned and grew an empire, all while my father wilted away to drink and depression. Now, for the first time, I don't hate him." His eyes misted.

Kat forced the rising hormones that threatened tears into submission. He needed her in this moment. "He's your father. You can hate what he did but still love him."

Her words stung with truth because of her tumultuous relationship with her own parents, but that was a subject for another day.

"It's worse than that." Tears broke free and ran down his chiseled jawline. She kissed each of them away.

"What is it, then? Tell me."

He swallowed and inhaled a stuttered breath. "I understand now because if I lost you, I'd face a darkness I never thought possible in this world, and to know that I caused it..." He sniffled and blinked away more tears. "I'd hurt so much that I'd blame the world the way my father blamed me. Even worse, how could I create a child who could suffer with me as his or her father?"

She threw her arms around his neck and held him tight. "Shh. You'll make an excellent father."

He broke in her arms. The man, the rock, the protector, opened up and showed his weakness to her, and she knew this was something he never showed anyone. She rocked him and held him tight as his body shook. Shook from love. Shook from hope. Shook from terror.

Wes crumbled in Kat's arms like a little boy, and he hated himself for it. He needed to be the one to hold her up, to keep her safe. He managed to regain control of himself and sit up tall. More than anything, he wanted to escape the pitiful look he knew he'd find in Kat's eyes. He pried her arms free from around his neck but kept his attention on the sky. "We need to go inside."

"Don't." Kat pressed both hands to his face and forced him to look at her, but he didn't see pity in her eyes. "I love you more than I've ever loved anyone. And in this moment, I know for a fact you are the only man I could ever love. You're everything to me, and you're the only man I'd ever want to have a baby with. Together, we can do this. Together we can do anything."

She sat up and fisted his shirt, yanking him to her. Chest to chest, lips to lips, she kissed him like he'd never been kissed in his life. His skin seared with want and his heart ached to be closer to her, so he forgot himself and pulled her tighter.

Raindrops dribbled from the sky, but it didn't cool his body. Thunder clapped in the distance, and he didn't care. Like the rain rolling in to land, his desire rolled over his fear, and he plummeted into the icy waters of acceptance. He wanted Kat, and he wanted this baby.

A boom sounded, and the world shook underneath them. His protective nature won over, and he broke the kiss. They panted in each other's arms. Rain pelted them. He heaved until he caught his breath again and shook off his foggy thoughts.

Kat shivered, and he shifted into action, picking her up and carrying her inside to the master bathroom, where he set her on her feet. He turned on the bathtub faucet. The clinking of old pipes and the gush of water covered the claps of thunder outside. "You need to get warm."

"I'm fine. Promise. Go get changed, and we can enjoy an evening together."

He eyed his watch. "Isn't the gang due here soon?"

"No, I told them I wanted an evening for just the two of us."

Her words were like the soothing cream she'd used on his sunburn. "Sounds nice. I'll be right outside the door if you need anything. Toss your wet clothes out, and I'll put them into the wash."

"You spoil me."

"I enjoy this. Even if I might have turned one of your nightgowns pink."

"What?"

He toed the floor, droplets splashing to the tile, so he grabbed a towel and mopped it up so Kat wouldn't slip. "Don't worry. Won't happen again. I watched a video on how to do laundry. I'd never done mine before."

She laughed. "Of course you haven't."

He backed from the room and pulled the sliding door to an inch from being closed then went to change.

The storm beat through town, with high winds scraping tree branches to windows and an occasional lawn chair or trash can lid flipped by. After the clothes were in the washing machine, he went to the kitchen to fix some chicken tacos and rice.

Kat entered with her damp hair pulled up, showing her lean, long neck. "Wow, it's really blowing out there."

Lightning flashed, thunder boomed, and the lights flickered.

"Smells delicious. I didn't know that you were such a good cook."

He set the plates down on the counter, took milk out of the fridge, and poured a glass for each of them. "Wasn't. More videos. Funny, I didn't know that cooking could be so relaxing. I enjoy it. Maybe I should open a restaurant in town or something."

The lights flickered again. "I think it's a great idea for you to find something to occupy your mind and attention, but opening a restaurant in this town wouldn't be easy. Cassie put two others out of business already. The woman is ruthless."

"I'm not sure I'd want to be gone all the time running a business like that anyway. I need something I can do from out of the house if I'm going to be raising a child with you." He shrugged. "Besides, I've been busy looking into grants and funding for people who need it. Did you know there's a grant somewhere that I read about online that will help cover the costs of all the therapies for a child with severe challenges?"

"That's good, right?"

Irritation nibbled at his neck. "Yeah, except for the fact that I read in the forum that people are having to pay a thousand or more dollars to have someone fill out the paperwork for them. That's ridiculous."

"Sounds like you might have found something you're passionate about."

He stirred the chicken in the pot. "Maybe."

The lights flickered then conked out completely.

"Do you have any lanterns or flashlights?"

"I've got something better." A match struck and sizzled, and then candles at the dining table flickered and torched to life.

"Perfect," he said. They settled in at the table and ate by candlelight. "Who knew milk and tacos could be so romantic." He enjoyed the peppery flavor and hoped it wasn't too much for Kat. Based on the way she ate every bite, he guessed she really was feeling better.

For a few hours, he dared to believe the sun would come out again and everything would be okay. Kat did that for him. She made him believe he could have it all.

Her and the baby.

Chapter Nineteen

KAT EYED the calm water and the leaves blowing in the wind nearby. "What a perfect day for sailing."

Trace and Dustin handled the lines from the dock while Trevor stood at the helm. Jewels packed things away so they wouldn't roll off the counters, and Wes unzipped the stack pack. No one would let Kat stand while the boat moved, so Wind sat nearby as a constant guard.

Great. Now Kat had six mother hens. She sighed and leaned back in the shade while everyone else worked. It was a great opportunity to drill Wind for her snide remarks and strange behaviors in the recent weeks. "So, how's it going?"

"The men are pounding their chests and the women are following orders. Of course, I'd include Trace as one of the men. Are we ever going to get that girl to cut her hair?"

"I'm not talking about the others. I'm talking about you."

"Good, as long as you remain seated and do what you're told like a good little girl." Wind wagged a finger at her.

"Not me. You. Spill it, girl. Did you hit menopause and the hormone monster took over your personality?"

"You're one to talk... Preggo hormones have done a number on you," Wind chided back at her.

Kat lifted her sunglasses and looked at Wind so she'd know how serious she was. "Who is it, and do I need to have Trace hire someone to take him out? You know I'm the girl to bury the body for you."

"Please, you couldn't even lift a shovel right now." Wind waved her off, but Kat never let an argument go without a proper rebuttal.

She lowered her glasses onto her nose and crossed her arms. "You're captive the next several hours. You can tell me now or in front of the rest of the crew."

Wind shot straight. "You wouldn't."

"I would."

"In front of the men?"

"In front of the world, so spill it, girl. I'm feeling more like my old attorney self, so share the dirt."

"I think I liked you better as a crybaby." Wind leaned back and put her hands behind her head, looking up at the covering to block the sun in the cockpit. "Fine. Man, yes. Problem, yes. Do I need help, no."

Kat put on her attorney hat and sat forward, tapping the table that stood between them. "Is it Damon Reynolds? Someone else? Do you have a new man?"

Wind didn't answer.

"Now or in front of the rest."

"Fine. Yes and no. Man, yes. My man, no. When I'm ready to talk, you'll be the first I tell."

The others returned, and Wes took his place by Kat's side while Trevor motored them out through the river to the ocean. Wes winked at her as if to let her know the secret he'd already told her about the proposal was on its way. Was this his way of warning her he was going to follow suit and get down on one knee on the beach?

"What are you two whispering about over there?" Wes asked.

Dustin shot an over-the-shoulder, you-betrayed-me look at Wes, so Kat quickly covered since she didn't want to confess that Wes had broken the man code. "Baby stuff."

"Okay, we can't wait another minute. Please tell us what the doctor said."

Wes stood up and took out the picture of the baby from his pocket. She didn't know he'd brought it, but the way he showed it around with the biggest boyish grin on his face made Kat think this new direction in their lives could be better than their original plans.

The girls squealed, while the men patted him on the back and congratulated him.

Wind glanced at the picture. "Looks like an alien."

"Jealous much?" Trace accused.

Wind had a way of being bitter but still making someone feel loved. Kat wasn't sure how she did it, but

Wind had a talent for telling you off but making you feel special all at the same time.

"When can we set up the shower for you both?" Jewels asked.

A wave rocked the boat, so Wes put a protective arm around Kat. "I thought a shower was a girl thing," Wes said.

"Not at our age," Kat teased. "We need everything, so we'll register and work together."

"Okay, but we can't for a couple of weeks. We're not out of the storm yet. In two weeks, if all is well, we can start telling people."

"This is about to get interesting. Rhonda is going to have a field day with the rumors. Best make a direct call to STSB before you tell anyone so you can control the narrative," Jewels said.

"Not kidding," Trace added. "Best tell your mother before word gets to her."

Kat cringed from the comment. Being pregnant and unmarried was one thing. Facing her mother would be an entirely different level of stress.

Wind shot up. "Look, dolphins!"

The girls flooded to the front of the boat to sit on the trampoline and watch the dolphins play in the water in front of the bow of the boat.

Jewels leaned into Kat. "Did he ask again?"

The girls all stared at her as if they'd extract the information through osmosis.

"No." Kat didn't want to talk about the three times so

far she'd thought he was going to propose and was left feeling rejected. That was how she'd made him feel all those times.

"Perhaps you need to tell him it's okay now or something," Wind offered.

"Maybe he hasn't had the right moment," Trace added.

Kat toyed with a loose strand of rope. "We had a candlelight dinner last night when the lights went out. It was romantic and beautiful and perfect, but no proposal. I thought maybe..." She caught herself before she spoke the words.

Trace patted her knee. "You thought he might follow Dustin's lead and propose on the beach today."

Jewels and Wind screeched in a higher pitch than the dolphins.

Trace swatted at them. "Don't. He thinks it's a surprise."

"How'd you find out?" Kat asked.

"You knew, too?" Wind scowled.

She shrugged, not wanting to give away her source. "I guessed. How did you figure it out?"

Trace smiled. "We use the same computer, and he searched how to propose to an activist in Florida."

They all laughed. "Really?"

"Yep, and let's just say I'm glad he didn't try to ask me while riding on the back of a stingray in scuba gear. I guess there's some positives for the man I love being scared of the ocean. I told him I didn't want a fuss." She turned to Kat. "So you think Wes's going to follow suit?"

"I hope so. I'd like to have the wedding before the baby comes. I thought after last night—"

Wind elbowed her in the side. "Last night, huh?"

Kat rolled her eyes. "When he shared his fears with me about the pregnancy, becoming a father, and losing me. He opened up and showed a vulnerable side I'd never seen."

The wind picked up at the end of the river where they merged into the ocean.

Jewels secured her hair behind her neck with a tie. "That must've been hard for him to express. He's such a proud man."

"It was. It made me feel special. Like he finally completely trusted me with his truth."

"And does he know yours?" Trace asked.

"My truth? What's my truth?"

All three women looked to each other.

Jewels chuckled. "I guess you haven't read my message yet."

Wind huffed. "That's what you wrote. Well, it's no secret that Kat's scared of being a mother because of how her mother raised her and how she feels like she doesn't possess the motherly instincts needed to care for a child."

"I see." Kat twisted the strand of rope around her finger and eyed the open ocean ahead. "You're right."

Dustin and Wes climbed to the roof and did something to the sail then returned to the cockpit. A second later, the material rose and filled like a parachute. Engines cut off, and they coasted through the channel. For the first time in days, her stomach protested at the rocking of the boat, but she managed to keep down her breakfast all the way to the island.

When they were anchored near the shore of a stretch of beach no bigger than an oversized sandbar, Kat welcomed the short swim to land. The minute she entered the water, her stomach settled. Wes swam by her side with a waterproof bag over his back. "Got sunscreen in that bag?"

"Three bottles." He turned on his side and watched her swim to where she could touch, and then they stood in the surf and kissed while the water lapped against their legs.

"Hey, you two. Stop playing fish face and come have some lunch," Dustin shouted.

Wes took her by the hand. "I think this is the big moment. You ready?"

Her heart fluttered and her pulse quickened, as did her steps. "Absolutely."

This was it. The proposal he'd been waiting to give her. That was the reason he'd told her about Dustin and Trace. He was gauging her reaction to the idea. "I think this is so romantic. A perfect place for a proposal," she encouraged him.

"Based on what I know about Trace, I agree."

They made their way to the end of the beach, and the gang dropped back from Dustin and Trace. He took her to a piece of driftwood and sat her down then lowered to one knee, ring out. Wes tugged Kat back to his side, where they stood watching.

Jewels glanced at Kat with pressed lips and an I'm-sorry gaze but then returned her attention to Trace. Kat brushed off her hope and watched as her dear friend listened to Dustin pour his heart out to her. She could only catch a few words from this distance, but she heard something about his life beginning the day they met and how she challenged him and how he couldn't imagine a minute of his life without her in it.

Trace nodded, and he slipped the ring on her finger. Everyone cheered.

Kat forced her disappointment to remain hidden and enjoyed the afternoon by a campfire cooking some fish and veggies. They all sat around, and Wes leaned in to whisper, "You feeling alright? I can get Dustin to take us back."

"I'm good." Kat looked to her friends for help.

Wind picked up a stick and stirred the glowing embers. "She's probably realizing that her life is about to change."

"I've been thinking about that." Wes rubbed his thumb against her palm. "We have plenty of money, so we can do everything we want. We can hire a nanny and staff to help out."

The girls all stood stone still and looked at Kat. That's when she realized Wes's non-proposal was a blessing. Despite how he'd opened up to her, they hadn't faced any real challenges. She needed him to know what was non-negotiable here and now. "I won't have my children raised by staff."

"I didn't mean we'd abandon our child. I only meant that we could still be free when we wanted."

Kat faced him, her anger and resentment bubbling to the surface. She'd been caught up in hormones and dreams and happily-ever-afters. But that wasn't reality. "That sounds like abandonment to me. But my parents labeled it as vacations and business trips. How will you label it?"

Chapter Twenty

THE SAIL back to the docks was uncomfortable. Wes focused on learning to sail, finding it a good outlet for his confusion and stress. The way Kat had looked at him speared his heart. What was she so upset about? He'd thought they'd made progress.

He allowed the women to hang together on the trampoline to no doubt discuss his ineptness as a boyfriend and soon-to-be dad. Dustin handed him a rope to flake, a term he'd learned only a few minutes earlier. "I wouldn't take it personally. Women are difficult to figure out sometimes."

"All's good. Today is your day. I'll figure out how to make Kat understand I wasn't trying to abandon my child or her."

"It isn't my place to interfere, but since I'm a Manster, I think I have a pass," Dustin teased.

Wes felt a connection to Trevor and Dustin he hadn't felt with the acquaintances of his past. He'd always maintained a healthy distance from people, but these men weren't having it. "Go ahead."

"I don't think it's you leaving her she's worried about. If I understand it right, from what I hear, Kat never saw her parents."

"I know that, but I didn't realize it made her so bitter."

"I think it's more than that. Trace mentioned something about her not knowing how to raise kids. Maybe she fears she won't be a good mother?"

A light went on in Wes's dark man-brain. "She fears she's going to be just like her own mother."

Wes strung the rope over the lifelines and tucked it through so it would stay the way the men had shown him when they had left the dock. "I'm sure we can talk it through tonight." He didn't like the distance he felt from Kat after their connection yesterday.

He didn't know why these men drew out further thoughts, but Wes shared even more. Maybe he needed to vent to someone he couldn't hurt with his words. "I have to confess, though. This journey has been exhausting. All I want is for these next two weeks to be over, and then I can relax a little. If the doctor is right, we'll be mostly out of danger at that point. It'll be good for us to have some time thinking about what's next. I've been stuck between accepting the pregnancy and worrying about Kat suffering physically to carry the child. I've never liked seeing a woman suffer, especially not her." That's when Wes knew they needed to start making plans for the future, but he wasn't ready. Something held him back.

The boat docked, and they unloaded their gear and headed to Trevor's, but Kat tugged on his sleeve. "Sorry, guys. I'm tired. I need to call it for the day. Congrats, Trace. I'm so happy for you."

He heard the lack of enthusiasm for Trace's happiness, despite Kat's forced smile, and based on the girls' reactions, they heard it, too.

"Get some rest," Jewels said.

The girls swooped in for a hug, and then as if to pass her off to him, Wind took her hand and placed it in Wes's. "Take good care of her." It was more than words. It was a gesture to let him know that he'd been accepted into their family.

They walked hand-in-hand to Kat's large home a few blocks away.

"Did I do something wrong?"

She shook her head but didn't look at him. "No. I'm tired."

They reached their front door, and he stopped her on the porch, turning her in his arms. "You don't have to talk now, but in two weeks when everything's all clear, it's time for us to make some plans."

She raised a brow and stepped into his space. "What kind of plans?"

"That's what we should discuss." Wes tucked Kat's hair behind her ear and admired her perfect complexion, full lips, and beautiful eyes. "I'm looking forward to waking up and seeing this face every morning for the rest of our lives."

She stepped closer, her hands moving to his hips. "You are?"

"Yes." He kissed her forehead and pulled her into a hug. "Let's get through these last two weeks, and then we'll figure out our next steps together."

He felt her tense in his arms but had no idea why. If only she'd come with a manual.

For the next two weeks, she remained cordial and followed all the doctor's instructions. The gang dropped in and out for dinners and game night but never stayed longer than a few hours, and they always called first. Wes appreciated the respect and tried to make them feel welcome any time they came over. But the more things developed into something solid with his new friends, Kat moved further away, and he knew if he didn't do something soon, he could lose her forever.

The morning of the official end of their first trimester came. Kat sat straight up in the chair a foot away from him, her hands in her lap. He'd given her space, believing it was what she needed while waiting for the final results of her tests and sonogram. But he longed to feel that connection like the one they had that night on the rooftop.

Dr. Ryland entered the office, and per her usual unorthodox ways, she pulled a chair up to them and sat forward as if they were going to play a game...but this was no game. "I won't keep you in suspense. We've already discussed all the risks, and you're aware of the possibility of a child with unique needs."

Kat hugged herself. "Doesn't matter. I'm not going to terminate out of fear that my life could be more challenging because I need to love a special child."

Dr. Ryland offered a sincere smile. "I applaud you both. And knowing this about you, I'm happy to share that your baby appears healthy and your pregnancy is going well."

Wes let out a breath of worry and confusion that had been building for three weeks. His muscles relaxed to a point where he could feel his hands and feet again.

"I've informed the specialist that you are opting not to have the amnio."

"What did he say?" Wes asked.

Kat shot him a sideways glance, her arms tightening around herself.

"I'm asking not to determine the baby's health, but Kat's."

She relaxed and looked to the doctor.

"Mother appears to be healthy. Her blood pressure is down. Sugar levels are great. Everything appears to be good. Whatever you're both doing, keep it up."

A shot of happy juice plunged into him. "This means we're out of danger? That Kat and baby are well?"

"We can tell people now?" Kat asked.

"Yes. Just continue with all the instructions I gave you. Healthy diet, exercise without overdoing it, avoid stress, and take your vitamins." She patted Kat's hand. "You're doing so well."

Kat sat a little taller, and Wes saw the spark return in her eyes. As he'd suspected, she had been stressed waiting for the all-clear. That's why she'd been so distant. Now they could move on and plan their lives.

Still, that pinprick of worry sent pins and needles over his skin. One trimester down, two to go, and then the delivery. He wouldn't think about that right now, though. He'd hold on to this good news and cling to it for a while.

They left the office feeling lighter, and when they returned to the house, for the first time in weeks she snuggled up to him while he read about her second trimester. He closed the book and pulled her against him, savoring their connection. When had he become so needy? He didn't care. "How you feeling?"

"I thought we were in the clear." Kat ran a finger up and down his chest as if studying the wrinkles in his T-shirt.

"We are. It was a general question." He stroked her hair, enjoying the smell of Freesia. A flower he only recently discovered after reading her shampoo bottle. "You've been distant lately, but you haven't told me why. Can we talk now?"

She sat up. The rigidness of her spine and her downcast gaze told him she was about to drop an island-sized worry on him.

Kat studied her nails.

Wes's patience wavered. "Since when do you avoid an

argument? Where's my Kat? The woman who challenges me at every moment of every day? Stop holding back. Whatever I did, I can't fix it if you don't tell me."

A flicker of fight shone in her tightening jaw. He cleared his throat and readied for an assault of emotions. "Is it about hiring staff to help with our child?"

She pushed her shoulders back, and the courtroom cougar showed her teeth. "I'm not going to run away from my child. You can. I know you didn't want this baby."

"That's not fair." Wes threw his hands up. "I needed a minute to face the idea of having a baby, but I've been by your side this entire time."

"Yes, but what about when the baby's born? Are you going to run off and leave him or her with staff?"

He took in a deep breath, thankful the men had talked him through this a bit before now. "Listen, I only tried to show that we can be a family and still have alone time, but that doesn't mean I don't want our child."

"I won't abandon my son or daughter while I run off to play on white-sand beaches and fly across oceans. Having therapists and doctors to help is one thing, but I won't hire a nanny so I can escape raising my child."

"You're not your mother. You'd never make your child feel unwanted. But having a nanny to help isn't a sin or a sign of bad parenting. If I end up starting a company or organization, how'll you work if we don't have help in the house?"

She opened her mouth but then closed it, so he continued to drive his point further. "Don't you see we're in this together? We both want the same things, so what's the problem?"

"You don't love me," she blurted. "Not enough to marry me."

His mouth fell open, but there were no words. He looked from the window to the floor to her face to find the answer. "Why the heck would you say something like that?"

"Not enough to want to marry me now that I'm having your child." Kat pushed from the couch and escaped to the bay window.

He wouldn't let her go that easily. "What are you talking about? I've only asked you a dozen times. I've made a fool out of myself trying to get you to say yes."

"I never asked you to," Kat said in only a whisper.

"Face me, Kat. If you want to accuse me of not loving you, then you better face me to do it."

She turned, lifted her chin, her lips tight. "You proposed before, but not now."

He threw his hands up. "Seriously? I flew here, got down on one knee, and held up a ring for the world to see. Only to be ushered inside by a friend and told to put the ring away."

"You know it's more than that. Maybe we're both too damaged to want marriage and family. Your father did a number on you growing up, and my mother showed me marriage was more business than affection."

"You're right. My father only showed me that parenthood was bitterness and resentment and loss and hardship.

But he was alone. And from what you said, your mother didn't marry your father for love. We have each other. We love each other. That means something."

"Then why haven't you proposed since you found out about the baby?"

"And when could I have asked you since then?" Wes ran a hand through his hair and paced the floor, willing his temper to settle before this got out of hand. But he was mad. Mad that she'd accuse him of such a thing when all he'd done is show her how much he loved her in everything he'd done.

"The night on the rooftop deck. The beach with Trace and Wes, the boat, the car, the doctor's office. I don't know. Anywhere. Before you found out about the baby, all you talked about was marriage, and it's the only thing you've avoided since you found out."

Wes wanted to get down on one knee now and tell her to marry him, but he wouldn't. Not like this. "How was I supposed to know you wanted to get married after you refused me so many times? You said you weren't ready. Are you ready now? If I got down on one knee, what would you say?"

Kat put her hands on her hips and took two steps forward, facing him nose-to-nose. "I don't want a pity proposal. No, I don't want to marry you."

Chapter Twenty One

LIGHT DANCED atop the surf surging into the lagoon of Friendship Beach. Kat rested her head back against the large, painted wood chair and sipped her nonalcoholic strawberry daiquiri. Relaxed, she closed her eyes and imagined playing in the sand, building castles and burying her little girl or boy waist-high. She swore she could hear the giggles of her little one in the wind sliding between palm leaves.

Her hand rested on her now-showing belly. Two months since the sonogram had gone with no issues. She wanted to rush to the end where she held her baby in her arms yet also wanted the time to slow down so she could enjoy each moment of growing a life inside of her.

"Is the baby kicking?" Jewels asked.

"Not that I can feel with my hand. Is that wrong?"

"No. I only asked because you were holding your belly," Jewels said.

"It's funny. When I first found out I was pregnant, I couldn't imagine being a mother. All I could think about was how this would disrupt our lives, but now..."

"Now you're attached and couldn't imagine not being a mother." Jewels sighed and looked up at the clear sky. "It's natural. As women, we get to connect before the fathers do. It's a gift."

Kat didn't have words to describe the connection she felt, but she knew she loved her child.

Jewels looked to the other girls. "We need to head back soon. The men will be meeting us at Kat's. You know if we're late, Wes will be pacing the floor, worried about mama and baby.

Trace slurped the last of her red slush. "Has Wes calmed down? The men said he still worries about you all the time."

"He's been better about letting me breathe." She didn't want to say he gave her more than a little space, more like there was a hundred-foot valley between them. Nothing had been the same since she'd accused him of not wanting to marry her.

"You ladies are being too nice." Wind huffed and unceremoniously dropped her plastic glass into her chair's cup holder and leaned forward. "Why'd you tell Wes that you'd tell him no if he asked you to marry him again?"

Kat swallowed a gulp of her drink down the wrong pipe, choking on the seeds and the realization that Wes had shared their relationship drama. "What? Where'd you hear that?"

"From the Mansters," Wind huffed.

"They still calling themselves that? How silly." Kat shook her head and pointed at the surf. "Look, I think that's Rhonda. She's probably got a spyglass pointed this way, taking notes on our time here. Rumors are already spreading about my man, and I'm sure someone's noticed my belly bump."

"Nice conversation detour, but I'm ramming the barricade. Talk." Wind closed her cover-up around her waist and turned to face Kat with all the stage drama she could muster in one motion. "You know, you're knocked up and fifty. Not sure you're going to find another man at this point."

Jewels rose from her chair and opened the cooler as if their conversation delayed their departure. "Wind, behave."

She shrugged. "Telling the truth is all. Kat knows that. How many times has she berated me with the truth?"

"Put a straw in it." Trace shot her a shut-your-mouth glower then turned to Kat. "Still, Wind has a point. Wes is a good man. He loves you. You love him. Why won't you marry him?"

Kat wanted to avoid this line of questioning. "I think I'll go for a swim."

"You can't outswim me, so start talking," Trace said, and it was the truth. No one could outswim her.

Jewels pulled out the pitcher of daiquiri and poured more in each of their glasses. "We only want to help you. If there's a reason you don't want to marry him, we will respect that. Heck, we'll run him out of town now. But if you're avoiding marriage out of fear, then you need to talk about it."

Kat buried her toes in the sand, the bright-blue polish showing through the grains as if water had seeped up through the ground. "Think about it. He tried to ask me up until he found out about the baby, and then he didn't ask me again."

"Yes, but he told the men that he hadn't had a chance. That he was so worried about you, he hadn't even thought about proposing. He didn't want to add any more stress to what you were already going through."

Kat was both happy Wes had bonded with the other men and equally annoyed that he shared like a thirteen-year-old girl. "I know what he said, but now that we know the baby is going to be a permanent part of our lives, I can't figure out if he wants to marry me now out of obligation or because he wants to."

"That's the hormones talking." Wind waved her hand at Kat. "You know even with that baby bump, you're beautiful, smart, and bossy."

Kat laughed. "Not wrong. I'm as bossy as you are theatrical."

"Not wrong." Wind winked. "Anyhoo, do you want to lose an amazing guy like Wes, the father of your baby, because you're scared he's only proposing out of obligation?"

"You don't understand." Kat pulled her hat down

lower on her forehead, shielding her skin from the dark-spot-generating sunrays.

"Yes, we do. You think because your mother and father were so unhappy and were never around, that's how it'll be for your child. You think it would be easier to be on your own than with Wes, who wants a life beyond parenthood."

"Yes. You heard him that day. Wes said he would hire staff to care for our baby. He says that is only to give us a break, but I can't help but worry he'll want a life beyond parenthood. He's been a bachelor for fifty-two years. I won't do it. I won't abandon my child like that. He won't admit it to me or himself, but Wes wants a life I can no longer give him, so if we get married, he'll only resent me someday. I love him too much to trap him like that. I won't end up like my parents."

"Talk to him, Kat. Tell him all of this," Jewels urged.

"He'll only tell me that I'm wrong and he won't even consider my words. Wes carries his own baggage. He thought he'd never be a father. He never wanted to get a woman pregnant because his father accused him of killing his own mother when he was born."

Trace abandoned her drink as if the conversation took too much concentration to be distracted with an icy beverage. "That's harsh."

"And he also told Wes that if he ever got a woman pregnant, the same would happen to her."

Kat's heart ached at the thought of him worrying about something so ridiculous. "He thinks he'll be no better than his own father, who ignored and belittled him growing up."

"Wow, no wonder the guy's so scared." Wind looked at her nails and then at the sand. "You realize you're one lucky girl to have a man who would give up his life's plans to stay home and have a baby with you. A man who would sacrifice anything to be with you. A man who cares more about you than himself. A man who loves you."

"But he won't love me forever."

"Kat, your parents treated marriage like a business arrangement. Your relationship with Wes is different. That man loves you. The question is, do you love him?" Jewels would've made a good lawyer.

"Yes, I do. More than my heart can take sometimes," Kat said with no reservation at all. "But I love this baby more than I can express, and isn't it my job as its mother to protect him or her from a father who doesn't want to be there?"

"Doesn't want to be there or is scared to be there?" Trace asked. Kat couldn't help but notice Trace's overprotectiveness had faded into the shadows. Wes had done the impossible. He'd earned her trust.

"Isn't it the same thing?" Kat asked.

Jewels replaced the pitcher and closed the cooler. "No, it's not. Fear can tear us apart. Don't let it win."

"Sailing" by Rod Stewart echoed from Jewels's beach bag.

"No phones allowed, remember?" Kat scolded.

"It's off. It would only ding for a contact I have in favorites." She dug through her bag and pulled out her phone. “It’s Trevor. He wouldn’t call unless something was wrong.”

“Answer it, then.” Kat went to her side, hovering like Wes when it was time for her to take her vitamins.

“What’s wrong?” Jewels asked without a hello or anything. “No. Seriously?”

“What’s up?” Trace asked, already packing their stuff.

“On our way.” Jewels ended the call and tossed her phone into the bag. “The STSB reports seeing Kat’s mother arrive in town, and she’s on her way to the house. Your house.”

“But the men are there putting together the stuff for the nursery.” Kat grabbed her beach bag and raced for the dinghy. “We need to get there fast.”

The girls grabbed their stuff and raced to the boat, pushed off, and charged across the river to the docks at Trevor’s hotel. There was no time to waste. Not when Kat knew if there was anyone on earth who could chase Wes off, it was her mother.

When they unloaded and reached Jewels’s car, she paused and faced Kat. “I wish you had more time. But you better decide right now what you want from Wes. If not, you know your mother will decide for you.”

Kat huffed. “I’m a grown woman having a baby of my own. She can’t rule my life anymore.”

They all hopped into the car and raced the few blocks to her home. But when she saw her mother’s car parked in the driveway, her gut clenched tight as if the baby boxed inside her belly. Her pulse quickened, and her mouth went dry.

"I won't let her make me feel small or like a failure. I won't let her take charge." Kat straightened to her full height, slung her beach bag over her shoulder, and marched inside her home to find her mother circling like a shark about to capture prey.

She turned on her too-high heels and *tsk*ed. "Guess you've done it this time. Good thing I'm home to clean up your mess." She tossed her purse on the side table. "The scandal needs to be controlled. I blame you girls. Told you they'd be the downfall of you someday." Her gaze fell on Kat's belly. "And at your age. You're lucky I decided to come home."

Kat stepped forward, her heart beating faster than the baby's had sounded on the sonogram. "This isn't your home anymore. It's mine. I bought it."

"Ungrateful as always, I see." She turned to Wes. "Did you want a baby so bad you'd risk my daughter? I mean, she's too old to give birth. You trying to kill her?"

Wes dropped the hammer, and his skin went sheet white. Kat couldn't remain silent. All the progress they'd made talking through his pain drained from his body with one statement from her mother.

"You have no right to speak to Wes that way." She stormed forward, ready for a fight. Ready to take on the one person who always cut her down and made her feel worthless. "If you're going to be ugly to the father of my child, then you can leave."

She huffed. "You're kicking me out of my own house?"

"It's no longer your house. It's my home now." Kat forced herself to keep her hand from her belly, despite the deepening knot inside her. "A home I plan on building with laughter and love."

Jewels went to her side, Trace at her other

Wind stepped in front of them all. She waved her arm like a wizard about to cast a spell. "Mrs. Stein, I've held my tongue all these years, and if you took the time to get to know me, you'd know how difficult that's been, but I can't hold it any longer. You need to realize Kat can take care of herself."

Mother crossed her arms over her chest. "Obviously she can't. Look at this place. There are boxes everywhere." She pointed to all the crib and cradle and cuddly baby stuff stacked around the living area. "And where's the staff? You can't run a house without staff."

Kat pushed past her friends, past the pain of being unworthy of a mother's love, and marched forward. "I don't want staff raising my child. Unlike you, I *want* to be a mother." A sharp, searing pain shot around her belly. She doubled over and cried out. Her stomach cramped like a vise. "Baby!" she cried out, her knees hitting the floor hard.

Friends buzzed around. Hands touched her. Words sounded. But Kat couldn't speak or comprehend anything but the fact that she could be losing her baby.

Chapter Twenty Two

WES COULDN'T SIT STILL a minute longer. He shoved from the hard chair and paced the hospital waiting room with hands fisted and anger bubbling to the surface. Anger at Mrs. Stein, sitting prim and proper in a chair with no emotion, anger at the doctors for not telling Kat to take it easy more, anger at himself for risking her life from the start.

"The baby's going to be fine." Trever offered his empty words, but he was no physician.

Jewels stalled Wes's assault on the linoleum. "Kat's strong. She's going to beat this. Think about it. The woman is fearless."

"Except when it comes to that woman." Wes glanced at Mrs. Stein and couldn't hold his words back any longer. He needed to fix this. "It was you. You upset her. I knew Kat said you were distant and uncaring and all business, but I thought she exaggerated. Now I know better. You're as cold and sterile as this hospital." His words flew from his mouth, unlike his normal cordial, controlled demeanor.

"You don't know what you're talking about." Mrs. Stein didn't even bother to look at him.

"I know you stressed her out, and now she might lose the baby or even worse." He choked on his words and struggled to keep his temper from exploding, but in that moment, he realized one thing. Despite the bitterness toward fatherhood he'd clung to since he was a boy, he wanted his son or daughter now. He would do anything to protect his unborn child. "You should leave. I'll be the one taking care of her."

Mrs. Stein looked up through her faux lashes. "I won't leave. I can't."

Wes wanted to show her the door and help her through it, but no matter what he thought of the woman, this was Kat's mother. "You can leave." He cleared his throat and forced a cordial tone. "I will care for Kat."

"You can't."

"I can. I've been doing it this entire time. I've been to every doctor appointment, every sonogram. I've read all the books. I've cooked meals, done laundry, cleaned house. You weren't here to help. Kat didn't even want to tell you about the baby until next week when the shower invitations went out."

"I'm here now."

He fisted his hands and unfurled his fingers several times. His former-attorney experience kicked in, and he wanted to fight. He faced Kat's mother, but there wasn't a hint of intimidation in her expression. "She doesn't need you upsetting her again."

The woman stood, sliding her purse handle onto the crook of her arm. "I'll go get us all some coffee, but I can't leave. I'm the only family she has to make tough decisions if she needs them made."

If he didn't know better, he'd say there was a hint of pain in her eyes. Maybe he'd misjudged her. It didn't matter. All that mattered was protecting Kat. "I'm her family now."

"From what I understand, not legally. That means I'm the only one who can legally make the decisions." She patted his shoulder in a patronizing way. "I thought as a former attorney, you'd know that." She brushed past him and left the waiting room.

He collapsed, his face in his hands. "Dear Lord, she's right."

Trace plopped down next to him and gave him a strong, get-over-it tap to his back. "Listen. You're the baby's dad. You'll have a say."

"No, she's right. I haven't been a lawyer for a long time, but even I know that. I should've pushed Kat instead of giving her space, but every time we discussed the future, she would get upset. I didn't want to risk her health. Maybe there's a minister here in the hospital." He shoved from the chair again, but Dr. Ryland entered before he could leave the waiting room. "How is she?"

Dr. Ryland offered a warm smile. "The labor has stopped."

"Labor? But it's too early." He spun to look for reinforcements, to make the doctor see she was wrong, because no baby could survive being born this early, could it?

"Yes, it is, but we've stopped the contractions and she hasn't dilated. Her waters didn't break. I'm going to keep her here to monitor her for the night. Her blood pressure has gone up. Is she avoiding salt and getting plenty of rest? Any stress?"

They all looked to each other, but he was the one to spill the truth. "Yes, her mother arrived in town. They don't have a great relationship. Can I keep her from seeing Kat? I mean, she's the only legal family member."

Dr. Ryland put her hands in the pockets of her white coat. "Kat will only be seeing who she wants to see. Right now, only one of you is allowed in her room at a time, and you can only stay a couple of minutes. If she gets agitated, please leave. Ms. Wendy Lively, Kat's requested to speak with you first."

Wes couldn't help the feeling of rejection, but this wasn't about him, so he stood aside and allowed Wind to pass.

Mrs. Stein arrived and cornered Dr. Ryland. "What's my daughter's status? I'm her mother, so I should be the one informed. I've already sent for a specialist who will be flying in tomorrow."

Dr. Ryland straightened in an uncharacteristic domineering posture. "Mrs. Stein, I assure you she is receiving the best treatment possible and, more importantly, the treatment she's requested. You need to cancel your specialist because Kat doesn't want that, and since she is the patient and doesn't have any mental deficiencies, what she says will go in this hospital."

"We'll see about that. I know the chief of medicine, and I won't let anyone near my daughter who isn't the best." She spun in a fury of white hair and uppity attitude, but in that moment she wasn't the one Wes watched.

He nodded at Dr. Ryland with new respect.

"You're doing everything right, and you'll make an amazing father. Trust me. I've seen many families go through similar situations. You need to take care of yourself, too. Kat can only lean on you as long as you don't break. That's why I sent Wind in first."

"She didn't ask for her first?" Wes couldn't help the joy seeping into his voice.

"She asked for both of you. I chose to send in Wind first because if Kat saw you right now, she'd be as worried about you as she is about her unborn child."

"Why? I'm not the one in the hospital fighting for my baby."

She smiled knowingly. "Aren't you, though? Sure, Mama's in bed, but you have it worse. You're forced to stand out here and wait. A man like you isn't used to being helpless."

He ran a hand through his disheveled hair, realizing he hadn't showered today and probably looked like a wreck. "I didn't think I had a right to feel this way. It's just that I want to do something, but I can't do anything."

"But you can. And you and Kat have amazing people

to lean on. Use your support system. Let them lift you up when you can't stand anymore." She touched his bicep and offered him that soft-eyed gaze. "You're allowed to feel what you're feeling. Talk to your friends, and talk to Kat. She's tougher than you think."

A nurse called her away, leaving Wes reeling with worry.

With Kat's mother gone from the room and with the news that Kat was okay and hadn't lost the baby, his adrenaline faded and his muscles fatigued. He looked to his friends in the room and then collapsed into one of those darn waiting room chairs, allowing himself to crumble because he realized there were people around him who could support him without judging his weakness. And he needed all the support he could get right now.

Chapter Twenty Three

Kat sat up in bed, trying not to pull the darn IV from her arm. She inhaled the stench of bleach and blame. "I can't believe I let my mother get me so upset." She rubbed her belly.

Wind sat in the chair by her side holding her hand. "Girl, say the word, and I'll bury her body."

They laughed. Their childhood antics and empty promises provided a temporary tourniquet to her worry. "I know we banter, but you know I love you."

"I know. What's not to love?" Wind sat back and pointed at herself. "I mean, I am something special."

"You're something, alright." Kat play slugged her in the arm. "Is she still around?"

"Your mom?" Wind nodded.

"Did she fire my doctor and hire a helicopter to fly me out of here to some special hospital far away?"

"She tried, but that doctor of yours put her in her place." Wind fluffed her hair. "I like that woman."

"So do I." Kat looked to the door. "How's Wes holding up?"

Wind shrugged. "Do you want the truth, or will it upset you?"

"Don't coddle me, please. I can't take that anymore."

She nodded. "He's what you'd expect, considering your mother told him she was your only legal family therefore had control of your care and he had no rights."

"Ouch." Kat thought her chest hurt worse than her stomach. "Why does the woman want to pay to care for me but doesn't want to actually care for me herself? I've never understood."

"I wish I knew." Wind fidgeted with her nails the way she did when she didn't know what to say.

"You do know something."

"I overheard my mom on the phone one time. Something about your mother not trusting herself caring for you."

"Why's that?" Kat asked.

"Don't know. When I asked Mom, she told me it was none of my business and to stop being so nosy." Wind smiled. "But hey. You stood up to your mother. You were amazing."

"Yeah, until I was doubled over on the floor. I've never felt so weak in my life. And now I'm going to be on bed rest for a few weeks." She took a breath. "But I'll do it if that's what will keep my baby safe."

"Of course you will, because you're nothing like your mother. And Wes is nothing like his father. We are all our own people. Even if we wished we could be someone else at times."

Kat caught that look again, the one where the stage light went out in Wind's eyes. "Tell me what's going on with you."

Wind took her hand and squeezed it. "Not now. Just do me a favor and realize that the man out there loves you and would do anything to be with you. If you don't marry him, you'll spend the rest of your life regretting it. Trust me." She pulled away. "You need to get some rest and I know Wes wants to see you, so I'm going to go. Doctor's orders. Only one person at a time."

Kat wanted to get more info out of Wind, but she knew there would be no way while stuck in this bed, so she let her friend leave, knowing she'd corner her later. She'd figure out what was going on and help her fix it.

A few minutes passed before Wes appeared at the door. He stood there as if scared to enter without permission.

The sight of the fear in his eyes matched what was in her heart. A lump lodged in her throat, and she reached out for him. "I'm sorry. I'm so sorry I almost lost our baby."

Wes crossed the room in two long strides and took her into his arms. "Shhh. You're fine. The baby's fine. We're fine."

"Are we, though? I love you, Wes. There's no other man in the world I want to be with." She blubbered but didn't hate herself for it. Especially when he crawled into the small bed and cuddled her into his side, her head to his chest.

Wes pressed a kiss to her head. "We're going to be just fine. Because we love each other."

She wanted to say more, she pushed to say more, but the words came out in heaving blubbers. "When you lifted me up and rushed me to the car, I realized something."

He held her tighter as if he feared she'd slip away. "Shh. We can talk about it later."

She nudged him to let her sit up and face him. Because she had to say these words to his face. She cupped his cheeks and looked him straight in the eyes. "You have been there for me through this all, and no matter how strong I am, I can't get through this alone. I can't get through this without you. No. That's not it. I don't *want* to get through this without you. I don't want to get through life without you."

Tears formed in his eyes, and he kissed her. Kissed away the worry. Kissed away the regrets. Kissed away the fear. Best of all, he kissed her the way he used to before the pregnancy.

The machines bleeped and beeped. Wes broke the kiss and rested his forehead to hers. "We better stop before the nurses come running in here."

She wiped the tears from his eyes. She'd broken the man who'd never cracked, but now they could put each other back together. "I never knew love could be like this. That I would trust a man to hold me up in this world. It goes against everything I believe in, everything I was taught."

"We're holding each other up. And our friends are holding *us* up." He guided her back to his side, so she settled her cheek to his chest with a yawn. "What are we going to do about my mother?"

"You can hate me if you want, but that woman isn't coming near you if she's going to upset you like that again."

"I could never hate you. It was a shock to face her, but next time I'll be ready. I won't react that way. I won't let her have that power over me. Not anymore. Not when I need to protect my own child." She took his hand and pressed it to her belly. "As much as I want to work things out with my own mother, we're the only family I need."

The baby tapped her skin, and they both gasped. "Was that a kick?"

"Kick or punch, I'm not sure, but yes. I think our little one wants to meet you." Kat sat still, waiting for the baby to move again, but when he or she didn't, her eyes grew heavy and she rested back into the bed.

Wes stroked her hair. "Our little one wants to let us know he's with us."

"Yes, she does."

THEY ENTERED the house to find the boxes neatly stacked in the corner and the place spotless. Kat clung to him, her eyes wide. "Mother."

His agitation stirred, but he wouldn't let Kat see it. "Let me get you off your feet, and then I'll speak with her. Don't worry. I'll be calm and cordial, but I won't let her upset you."

She gave a quick nod and headed for the stairs. He walked by her side to their room and tucked her in. A squirt of orange spritz filled the air from the device he'd bought to help keep her calm. Magazines were stacked on the bed, television remote on top. "Don't get up without me. Promise?"

"I think I've heard that before." She pressed a finger to his lips. "But this time, I'm not going anywhere. I won't do anything to endanger our baby. Total bed rest for the next few weeks."

He left her safely in bed and pulled the door closed, took in a calming breath, and headed down the stairs. In the kitchen, he found a maid dressed in a ridiculous uniform scrubbing all the surfaces. Mrs. Stein sat at a table with paperwork spread out in front of her.

"Mrs. Stein, I appreciate your efforts here," he said in a friendly but stern tone. "I apologize for my harsh words, and I want you to know that I respect that Kat is your daughter. However, I won't allow her to be anxious or any stress to cause her more issues."

Mrs. Stein placed a paper neatly onto a stack, removed her glasses, and angled in the chair to face him. "This is why I didn't return to the hospital. I've been here getting things ready. The nursery has been painted, the bedding ordered, and I've hired some staff to take some of the load off you both."

"But Kat doesn't want people in the house," Wes argued but in a tone that brooked negotiation.

"I know you find me harsh and unloving, but despite current popular opinion, I do care about my daughter and what happens to her. Allow me to provide some help the way I know how while you tend to her other needs."

He scanned the clean room. What she proposed gave Mrs. Stein a chance to worm her way into their lives. Despite the fact he wanted her gone, he didn't have the energy to fight, but he would if it meant protecting Kat from more stress.

"By having staff, you'll be able to keep her company, take care of her, and plan for your future while I provide food, cleaning, and workers to keep up things around here. Trust me, that girl will not remain in bed without a chaperone."

"She promised this time—"

"Trust me, that promise will last a few days. Her mind cannot be idle, or she'll never be able to remain in that bed. Keep a close eye on her the way only you can."

He caught a hint of regret or jealousy in her tone, but he wasn't sure, and he couldn't argue with her logic. Playing housemaid grew tiresome, and she was right. Kat needed a chaperone, so he offered her his hand. "I accept that deal. As long as you don't bother Kat unless she asks to speak to you."

"Agreed." She shook on it. "Trust me. We're both

better off with me working to protect her and not mothering her." She studied him as if he were a strange piece of modern art. "I ask one thing of you."

"What's that?" He retreated a step, readying for battle.

"Don't marry my daughter until after the baby is born. I don't want you to do something you both will regret later."

"I love—"

"I know you both think you do," she said in a way that made him want to run from the room.

"You don't think she loves me?"

"I think she's wrapped up in all the baby stuff and thinks this would be the best arrangement for the child. There are many reasons people marry. Seldom are they the right ones."

He thought to ask what she meant, but that was between her and Kat. Besides, he needed to get back to check on her. His legs were weak from exhaustion, so he climbed the stairs slowly and slid into bed by her side to doze. Each time she moved, he shot up to see if she needed something, but he must've fallen asleep at some point, because he woke to her fingers running through his hair and a smile.

"You could've crawled underneath the covers. You look like Morticia Addams like that."

He rubbed the sleep from his eyes and rolled over to face her. "How you feeling? Any contractions?"

"No. They seemed to have stopped completely."

"Can I get you anything?" he asked.

"No. I wish I could take a shower or a bath, but she wants me to remain in bed except for bathroom breaks for the next few days. I might run you out of the room with my stench, though." She chuckled.

The light in her eyes flickered. He savored the glint of the old Kat, and he wanted more of her. "Wait here."

"Where else am I going to wait?" She winked.

He went to the kitchen and retrieved a large bowl, ignoring Mrs. Stein's inquisitive eyebrow raise. He returned to the bathroom for a washcloth and soap, and then he went to Kat's bedside. "It won't be a real bath, but we can get you refreshed a little."

"You're too good to me. You know that, right?" Kat tugged him down to the bed by her side. "I'm sorry for everything. The hormones, the crying, the anger, my mother. I guess I can see why you wouldn't want to marry this version of a woman."

He wanted to work things out between them here and now, but she looked pale and weak still. Her mother's words echoed in his head with warning. Had Kat changed her mind because she was pregnant? Was it hormones? Nesting, like he'd read about in one of the books?

They needed to talk to figure out if Kat wanted to marry him for love or because of some maternal instinct or because it was the expected thing to do.

Chapter Twenty Four

WES SAT NEXT to Kat on the bed and swiped the rough washcloth softly down her arm. His tender touch, caring gaze, and occasional longing glance at her belly made her feel more cared for than she'd ever known in her life.

Droplets clung to the edge of her skin like a light drizzle on a summer day. His attentive gaze traveled from face to neck to arm with each swipe. "Is this helping?" he asked.

"Yes, it's refreshing. Thank you." She wanted to drill him about their future, but he looked worn out from stress and lack of sleep. And he was right. They did need to wait until they were both stronger and rested before they spoke about marriage, but she yearned to talk about the baby. "Do you think we should come up with some names?"

His hand stalled, his lips parted, and he took in a quick breath. "Maybe we should give it a week or two. Make sure we are out of danger."

An internal struggle obviously raged inside him. She could see he wanted to touch her belly, connect with his child, yet run from the room all at the same time. That's why he didn't want to get married. He could only focus on survival at this moment. "Do you trust Dr. Ryland?"

"Yes, probably more than I've ever trusted any other doctor."

Kat didn't want to say the words aloud, but she knew he needed to hear them. "She says that even if the baby doesn't make it, I will. That I'm healthy and nowadays women don't typically die in childbirth."

He flinched and pulled away, but she grabbed his arm. "I promise you, I won't die on you. Not like that."

His hands shook. "You can't promise that."

"I'm stubborn, you know. It's the one thing my mother gave me that I find useful." She took his hand and placed it on her heart. "Do you feel this? My heart beats, and it isn't going to stop, because I love you too much."

He offered a curt nod, then slid away from her. "I think there's more to your mother than you realize."

"She isn't a power-hungry person who didn't have time for raising a child?" Kat huffed. "Don't tell me she's poisoning you against me already."

"No one could do that."

"She will if she can. It's as if my mother has never been happy so no one else should be happy. She's run off every boyfriend I've ever brought around her. I thought you were stronger than that, though."

He plopped the washcloth unceremoniously into the

bowl and faced Kat. "I should tell you that your mother and I reached an agreement."

Kat's skin burned with warning. "What agreement?"

"She'll remain downstairs and handle the house while I remain up here with you. Before you object, I've already agreed. I'm afraid as hard as I tried to enjoy being a servant of sorts, I don't. I've never even taken out my own garbage. Cooking wasn't bad—I kind of enjoyed that—but the rest can go to staff."

She stiffened, but he took her hand and kissed each knuckle. "Kat, Dr. Ryland told me that it's okay if I need help, too. That I don't have to take everything on. We're not going to get into it now, but a relationship means compromises. I know you don't want staff raising our child, but it doesn't mean we can't have help with the house."

Everything inside Kat screamed to send her mother away, to keep her servant mentality away from them, but she didn't want to leave all the work to Wes. He looked tired and needed rest, too. "Okay."

His eyebrow rose. "Really? No argument? No judgment? No questions?"

"I can cry if you want. I'm apparently developing a talent for that." She winked, longing to have some time off from the drama in their lives.

"No, we're good." A hint of a smile broke on Wes's face.

"If we can move forward planning for the baby... We need to have faith that all will work out. I don't want to live as if waiting for something bad to happen."

Wes stood, removed the towel from the bed, and retrieved the bowl. "I'll be right back with some lunch, and then we can hang out and look through the baby name book I picked up."

"You did?"

"Yep. I didn't want to get ahead of ourselves, but you're right. We need to move forward. The girls will be by tomorrow to check on you. That way you're not stuck with my ugly mug twenty-four-seven."

"I don't know. I've gotten used to seeing your handsome face around more lately. A girl could get used to this kind of attention."

"Good, because I have plenty to give." He left her in the room with her thoughts of a brighter tomorrow.

The baby kicked, and she wrapped her arms around her middle. "Don't worry. I'm going to be the best mother possible. I'll never abandon you for work or travel."

Wes kept his promise and returned with a gigantic baby book of names. They cuddled up together and flipped through. "What about Bruce?"

"No. Kids would call him Batman."

"What about Roxy? Sounds tough yet feminine."

"Roxy's a dog's name, or worse." He flipped through some more pages. "This would be easier if we found out the sex of the baby."

"Do you want to know?" Kat asked, not wanting to keep him from his wishes but also not wanting to find out.

"I don't know. You?"

She turned the page of the book and eyed the list of

outrageous names she could barely pronounce. "No. I want to meet our child the day he or she is born. I don't care what we have, as long as he or she is healthy."

"Okay, but we can't keep saying he or she, and since we don't know what to name him or her, let's use a generic name for now. How about Peanut?"

"Why, because the baby's so small?"

"No, because the baby has a tough exterior to protect it—you—and a soft, loving world inside to comfort it." He shrugged. "Besides, my grandmother told me once my mother called me Peanut when she was pregnant. Kind of makes me feel like she's here with us."

"Peanut. Okay. I can go for that." She flipped a few more pages. "Tell me about your mother."

Wes shrugged. "I don't know much about her except that she was nice and kind to others but wasn't a strong person."

"She sounds like she was a kind woman. And our baby will know us." She took his hand to her belly. "Peanut, meet Daddy."

He swallowed loudly but didn't tear up this time. Instead, he lit up like the morning sun over the ocean. "Nice to meet you, Peanut."

They spent weeks writing a long list of possible boy and girl names. A month on bed rest that slowly eased on restrictions. Mother remained on the ground floor as she'd promised.

Wes did everything for Kat, except propose.

On the first day of Kat's seventh month, they left the doctor's office feeling lighter and ready to take on the world. "Sounds like everything's going smoothly. No more preterm labor, and Dr. Ryland even encourages you to get up and move around more." Wes tucked Kat into the car and headed back to their place.

"I'm getting so big. You're not going to want to look at me soon." She rubbed her belly. "I feel like I'm stretched from New York to San Francisco."

His hand slipped to her belly. "I think you're the most beautiful woman in the world, and there is nothing sexier than you carrying my child. Pregnancy agrees with you. You've got a glow to your skin, and you look happy."

"I am." She glanced out the window. "Now that I'm better, you don't have to run interference so much with my mother."

"Actually, I don't mind. She's been helping me with something." Wes hesitated to tell her what he'd been working on when Kat napped each day, but if they were going to be together, he needed to share everything.

"I'm intrigued. What could you possibly have to work on with my mother?"

Wes turned down their street and eyed the driveway ahead. "You know how Dr. Ryland told us our baby might need special care?"

"Yes, but she also said that Peanut might be fine, and if not we have the resources to get anything we need for our baby."

"Right. That's the point. We're lucky. Do you remember me telling you before about how insurance doesn't cover a lot of things children need? That certain medicines for seizures are not covered, so parents are forced to give their children medications that have worse side effects? The more I dug into studying the various issues, the more I realized how many families can't afford what they need."

She circled her hand around her belly and stared out the windshield. "I knew our health care system could be challenging, but to deny a child what they need? That's barbaric."

"I'm glad you feel that way, because your mother's helping me navigate the politics of getting laws changed, setting up grants, and bringing awareness to our defunct health care system. Also, we're attempting to open a center in Cocoa Beach that provides elite care for financially challenged parents with special needs children."

Wes pulled into the driveway holding his breath and pushed the gear into park to face Kat's judgment on his insane plan. "So, what do you think?"

She studied her perfectly manicured nails—the girls had come over yesterday for a mini spa day—and then she looked up through her thick lashes at him. "I think you're the most amazing man I've ever known, and if it's possible, I love you even more. And I want to help."

He relaxed into his seat for a second. "You know, your mother has been extremely helpful. I've gotten to know her a little better."

"Be careful. That woman stings like a man-of-war on steroids."

"Seriously, Kat." He gripped the steering wheel, eyeing the front door. "Now that the doctor gave you the all clear, I think you should sit down and work some things out. She wants to be a part of the baby's life."

"She said that?"

"No, but I can tell. It's as if she wants to be but is scared to be all at the same time." Wes hopped out of the car, opened Kat's door, and helped her to stand. "I just want you to be happy, and I'll spend the rest of my days making sure that happens."

She grabbed onto both of his arms. "Since I'm doing better, perhaps it's time we speak about our future plans."

"I want to be with you always." He willed her to see that.

"Then why not ask?"

He leaned his forehead against hers and closed his eyes, willing an answer to surface. "Is it tempting fate if we marry before the baby arrives?"

She shook her head. "Sometimes we need to believe love is faithful."

"What if I don't want to challenge fate?" That was the ugly truth. He was a coward even now. As if he put a ring on her finger, it was an admission he wanted to spend the rest of his life together. The way his father had vowed to his mother before she died giving birth to him. It broke the man, the same way losing Kat would break him. But would he turn his back on his own child if that happened?

Chapter Twenty Five

THE NEXT DAY, Wes left to run a mysterious errand, and Kat decided it was time to face her mother. Dr. Ryland, although reminding her to take it easy, had lifted her bed rest restrictions.

She found her mother in her father's old home office working on something she was sure had to do with her father's next big political climb. They were healthy, but Kat didn't know why they still wanted to work at their age. "Mother?"

Her mother uncharacteristically dropped her pen, and her mouth fell open. She tossed her glasses down and bolted up. "What's wrong? You need me to call Wes to come home?"

"No. I'm fine. I just wanted to talk to you. Do you have a minute?" She rubbed her belly. "I'd like to know some things before my baby comes."

"Tea in the living room?" Of course her mother would want to have a formal meeting.

"Sure. As long as it's decaf."

"Of course."

Kat went and sat on the couch in the living room with a pillow to support her lower back, which had a dull ache in it.

Mother ordered someone around in the kitchen and then joined her. "Tea will be out shortly." She sat at the edge of the couch in a ridiculous suit she wore despite being in a house in Florida with no company. "You look well."

"Thank you. I feel good." Kat took in a lifelong breath of resentment and charged forward with her unanswered questions. "Why didn't you want me?"

Her mother's eyes shot wide, but then she adjusted her suit jacket and said, "I did." She opened her mouth, shut it, then opened it again. "I guess I need to tell you some things you obviously don't remember from your childhood."

Kat tilted her head as if she could see her meaning better. "What kinds of things?"

"You know your father and I didn't love each other in the traditional sense. We met in college, and our families thought we'd be a good match. I never questioned it. I knew I wanted to succeed in life and so did your father, so it all seemed to be the right thing to do. We'd planned on two children and a happy life together, but when you were two years old..." Her voice faded away, as did her gaze.

Kat scooted toward her. For the first time in her life,

she felt an opening to connect with her mother beyond designer handbags and social event planning.

Her mother lifted her chin high and blinked past what Kat thought must be tears, but she couldn't comprehend her mother ever crying. "The minute I held you in my arms, my entire outlook on life changed. I quit my job. I wanted to be the best mother, but I soon learned that wasn't where my gifts lay."

"I don't understand." Kat moved closer but didn't reach for her mother, in fear she'd run away from the conversation.

"That day I was showing you how to plant flowers in our garden. The phone rang, and I left you to watch a butterfly while I ran inside to answer it. Your father was calling to ask why I didn't take a job that was offered to me, one that was an amazing opportunity. I told him I wasn't ready to return to work, that you were still so young. We argued. He told me how I'd never be the mother I was trying to make everyone else think I was and I should return to helping him rise up in the political world." She rushed through the words as if they burned her tongue as she spoke.

Kat reached for her mother, but she leaned away and held up a hand to stay her. "Don't. I have to get this out." She closed her eyes and then opened them with that cold façade reappearing. "I returned to the garden, but you weren't there. You'd wandered off. To the pool." Her voice cracked. "You'd fallen in, and you weren't moving."

The maid entered and put the tray on the table but

quickly retreated at her mother's scowl. "Ambulances, police, newspapers all flooded in to see my failings as a mother. Your father had been right, so I stopped pretending to be a good mother and returned to work where I belonged, at your father's side."

Kat saw it. The truth of it all. Why her mother had been so unhappy and cold and lost. "Mother, that could've happened to anyone, and I'm obviously okay."

"Yes, Kat. Because I hired people to take care of you. I gave you a chance to grow up and be the amazing woman you've become because I didn't pretend to be your mother."

She grabbed the tea kettle and poured the light-brown liquid into each cup. "Now you know. You'll make an excellent mother, but you don't have to get married to be happy with your child. I don't want you to feel like you have to get married because it's expected of you the way my marriage to your father was expected of me."

"But I love Wes. Our situation's different. He supports me in everything. He sold his company so we could be together more."

Her mother stopped mid-pour. "He did what?"

"Don't you see? Wes isn't Father. He's loving and attentive and lifts me up. I'm sorry Father never did that for you." Kat took the offered cup from her mother and sipped the warm, minty tea. "I want to marry him, Mother. Not for the baby or for you, but for me. It's taken me a long time to feel worthy of his love and to realize that even though our lives have changed from what we'd planned, if he still wants to be with me, I want him as my husband."

"Then why weren't you already married?"

"I said no originally because I was scared that we had a relationship too much like..." She faded off, not wanting to be cruel.

"Like your father and me."

Kat nodded. "He asked me several times before I got pregnant, but he hasn't asked again since he found out about the baby. I'm not sure if it's because he still wants a way out, if I told him no so many times that he doesn't want to ask again, or if he's still scared we'll lose the baby and things won't be the same. I don't know. All I know is that I'm sick of being scared of losing him or this baby. I want to enjoy the time we have instead of worrying what tomorrow will bring."

"Since when did the daughter I paid others to raise ever back down from something she wanted?"

Kat set the teacup and saucer back on the tray. "You're right." She stood and eyed the spiral stairs. "I'm going to propose, and I know just where to do it. Will you help?"

Mother stood, smoothing out the wrinkles that had dared to form. "You want me to help?"

"Yes. I know we have a long way to go with our relationship. I wish you'd explained this to me years ago, but so much makes sense now. And more than anything, I want everyone to be around to help love this baby."

"As long as I'm not left alone with him or her, I'll be a part of the baby's life, or I'll pay someone else to be."

"Was that a joke? Did my mother just crack a joke?" Kat grabbed her by the crook of her arm, ignoring her stiffening frame. "Come help your daughter plan the perfect proposal for her boyfriend."

Her mother adjusted her oversized diamond earrings. "Why not? Everything else in this house is backwards."

Chapter Twenty Six

The evening sun faded to an orange glow, and the lights on the rooftop deck twinkled. "You ready for this?" Mother asked.

"I think so." Kat opened the box revealing the silver band she'd ordered from Keith, their favorite jeweler in Chicago. She pulled it out and spun it around to see the inscription etched inside. *Love is faithful.* She hoped he'd understand her meaning. They both needed to take a chance on each other.

The doorbell downstairs rang, but her mother waved a dismissive hand. "The maid will answer."

She put the ring back into its box and slid it into her dress pocket then straightened the bow at the empire waist that showed off her oversized belly. "Only another six weeks and our little joy will be here."

"How are you feeling today?" Mother asked. Despite the sterile tone she'd yet to soften, Kat knew she cared.

"I feel great."

The baby kicked like a European soccer player at the start of a game. She grabbed her mother's hand and placed it on her belly. "Here, feel this."

Mother snatched her hand away. "Nope. I'll help with all the logistics, but I'm no real grandmother. Trust me, you don't want me near that child."

"When are you going to stop punishing yourself for a mistake many mothers have made? I'm fine. My baby will be fine and better with a loving grandmother." Okay, loving was stretching it a little, but still.

"I don't make mistakes unless it comes to children." She about-faced. "I'll go greet our guests while I send Wes up to fix a broken light."

"There's a broken light?"

"Nope, but your plan to wait until after everyone leaves won't work. Too much stress for you and the baby. Wes would never forgive me if I let that happen."

"You like Wes, don't you?"

Mother waved a dismissive hand. "I respect him."

"That's an even bigger compliment."

Mother disappeared downstairs, leaving Kat to stir in her excitement and anxiety. She'd grown tired of waiting for Wes to ask, and heck if she was going to have Peanut without a father if she had anything to say about it. Her baby deserved the best of everything.

Footsteps sounded on the stairs, so she closed her eyes, took a long breath, and whispered, "Don't worry, Peanut. He'll say yes." She wasn't sure if she was reassuring herself or Peanut, but either way, she wouldn't lose her nerve. She'd never backed down from a challenge before, and she wouldn't now.

Wes strutted out onto the deck with his old swagger back. The man she'd fallen in love with had slowly returned over the last several weeks, but today there was something else. A glint in his eyes. "How's my baby mama doing?"

She swatted at him. "That's all I am to you now, your baby's mother?"

He swooped her into his arms and kissed her with all the passion he'd held back the last several months, leaving her breathless and dizzy. With his arms tight around her, he guided her head to his chest. His heart beat fast and furious, matching her own. "I love you, Kat."

Guests' voices carried up from downstairs in a muted echo. She needed to get moving if she was going to ask. Her mother was right. She needed to do it soon to avoid the stress of waiting. "The ocean is rough tonight. You can hear the surf all the way here."

"Storm must be brewing out there somewhere." Wes moved to the edge of the rooftop deck and looked down. "We need to put a security lock on that door."

"Not a bad idea, but you can't babyproof our lives, you know."

"I can sure try." Wes stood with his hands on his hips, face toward the sky.

Kat took her opportunity, and holding on to the back of a dining chair, she lowered to one knee, not an easy task with her too-big belly and lack of balance from all the bed rest. She quickly yanked out the ring box, opened it with shaking hands, and held it up. The way he had on her front doorstep that day. She now realized how vulnerable and open he'd been when he'd tried to propose. The wait for an answer was unbearable.

Her knee wobbled, and she thought she'd tumble over to her side. "Wes, turn around, please."

He turned, and his eyes shot wide.

"Don't say anything, please. Let me talk first." She swallowed and cleared her throat of any worry. "I know this isn't the future we had planned."

He opened his mouth and stepped forward, but she shook her head to stop him. "Please, if you don't let me get this out quick, the pregnancy hormones will make me a blubbery mess and I'll never finish saying what I want to."

Her voice cracked, but she channeled the inner strength she'd inherited from her mother. "You asked me to marry you so many times before I found out I was pregnant, but I hesitated on saying yes because all I'd ever seen from marriage was misery. You told me our lives would be different and you chiseled away my apprehension, but then the pregnancy came and I knew I didn't want to live a life like my mother—one of regrets and resentment—so I pulled away. You told me you wanted to be with me no matter what, but I didn't believe you because I'd never seen anything but heartache."

She swayed, and he raced to her, but she held up her hand. "I'm fine. I just...I'm overwhelmed with the feelings that have been bottled up for so long. I wanted to be anything but my mother in life, yet I became her. Strong, independent, a fighter. All great qualities, but not at the expense of love. You've shown me how to love. How to trust and allow someone into my heart. You've held my hair as I've been sick, carried me when I was too weak to walk, forgiven me for keeping secrets, loved me when I didn't want to be loved. You're my baby's father, my everything, and hopefully you're going to be my husband. You are the one man I trust more than anyone else in the world. The one man I know I can lean on and you won't let me fall."

Her voice broke, and he fell to his knees, taking hold of her arms as if to keep her upright.

"Wes Knox, will you marry me?" She sniffled but allowed her tears to fall down her cheeks, not hiding from how she felt another day longer.

He didn't say anything, his gaze searching her face.

"Don't leave a girl hanging. Will you accept my proposal?"

Wes's mouth curved into a tight grin. "No."

Chapter Twenty Seven

Wes studied the woman who'd become his entire life. Her lip trembled, and he realized he'd rejected her, so he rushed to explain. "I can't accept your proposal because I have one of my own." He'd spent all week planning the perfect proposal, but he didn't want to see the hurt in her eyes another moment.

A distant rumble of thunder warned of a storm, but he didn't care. He wouldn't worry about something he couldn't see because he could see Kat right in front of him. "I love you and want to spend the rest of our lives together. I struggled for so long about losing you that I forgot I had you now. I wanted to wait until you were stable with the baby, not because I wanted a way out if Peanut didn't make it but because I wanted to wait until we could make the marriage about us and not about the fear we both faced as parents. I worried if something happened to you, I couldn't open my heart to our child, that I would become my father, but I know now that isn't going to happen because this baby is partly you. I waited so long to find a woman I didn't even know I was looking for. I'd planned on never marrying or having children, but you shredded my fear and replaced it with joy. You, Kat Stein, are the most amazing, strong, independent, capable, and loving woman I've ever known, and you don't even know how special you are, which makes you even more beautiful."

She sniffled and inhaled a stuttered breath.

"I won't lie. I'm still scared of losing you, but I can't wait another minute to be your husband. I needed you to know how much I wanted this. I waited until tonight to give you this because I was so hung up on making your proposal memorable, perfect, but now I can see *you* make *life* memorable." He snagged the ring box from his pocket, took out the ring, tossed the box aside, and held it up to her finger. "We don't know what will happen, but I know I want to face it with you. I have faith in our love. And Kat, I love you."

"I love you too," she whispered.

He slid the ring onto her finger and kissed her.

Claps erupted from the doorway, snagging their attention from their personal—and apparently public—moment.

Kat showed him the inscription, and he nodded his agreement, so she slipped the ring on his hand that matched the one he'd made for her. "Keith?"

"I had it shipped here." She wavered, but he grabbed ahold of her.

"I think I need help getting up." She laughed.

Her friends rushed to her side, and he lifted her to stand. She showed everyone her ring. People flooded in around them, carrying baby gifts and wearing bright smiles.

Kat had insisted the town be invited since she believed they all were part of her family and she wanted her child to grow up around people who loved him or her.

Houdini climbed up to the pergola, chattering away at them.

Skipper set her gift down on the table and grumbled, “Should’ve had this soiree at Cassie’s instead of this hippy hangout rooftop.”

Nancy Watermore walked out to the deck holding a sage-colored box with a yellow bow. “Didn’t know how to wrap this since I wasn’t told if it was a boy or a girl.”

“We don’t even know,” Kat said, eliciting a snarky comment on her way by.

Cranky Mannie joined them, handing over a bat. “Don’t care if it’s a boy or girl. Needs to like baseball. I made it up here, but don’t know if I’ll get back down that fancy staircase.”

Old Lady Francie took him by the arm. “We’ll make it down together.”

“Great. You’ll break a hip, and I’ll break my neck.”

Rhonda shooed them forward and held out her own gift. Kat blinked in surprise.

“I know you didn’t expect me to show, but Trace told me I should. Now that we’re neighbors, I think we get along a little better. Perhaps with age comes wisdom.”

"Let's play pin the diaper on the baby," Wind hollered.

Kat laughed. "Apparently not for everyone."

Rhonda nodded and continued on, allowing more people to extend their congratulations. The party lasted too long, and Wes worried Kat was overdoing it, so when the clock struck nine, he ushered the few remaining guests out the door and returned to the living room, where Dustin and Trevor unboxed the crib and carried the pieces upstairs. Kat waddled up behind them with instructions in hand and her friends trailing behind toting shower gifts.

He looked to her mother, who remained near the entrance to the kitchen, but she wasn't about to interfere. "Don't you think you've done enough today?" He rushed after them.

"I'm not tired, and I need to get this crib together. We only have six weeks left, and there's still so much to do. I need to get these baby clothes washed and the bouncy seat and cradle put together, not to mention washing bottles and burpees."

Wes watched her zip around the nursery as if she'd consumed two cups of coffee instead of chamomile tea. "How about you sit down, and I'll take care of the crib with the men and the girls can wash the baby clothes. The maid can do the bottles."

"I think Kat's nesting," Jewels said, taking the crib instructions away and handing them to Trevor.

Wes nodded. "I read about that in one of the books, but still, she shouldn't overdo it." He ushered her to the glider he'd purchased after reading it was a soothing place for mama and baby.

Kat didn't remain seated, though. She hopped up and headed for the baby monitor box. Water gushed to the floor, and Kat froze.

They looked at each other. Her lip quivered again. "My waters."

Jewels jumped into action as the girls surrounded her. "It's okay, hun. Everything will be fine."

"It's too early," Wes managed to mumble, but with one glance at Kat's tight jaw, he pushed aside his worry and focused on what she needed. "But Dr. Ryland said the baby would be fine now."

Dustin brushed past them. "I'll get the car."

"I'll call Dr. Ryland." Wind ran from the room.

Wes lifted Kat into his arms and walked down the steps. "It'll be okay, my love. Everything will be fine." He said it over and over again, trying to convince himself more than Kat.

By the time he reached the bottom step, she moaned and wiggled in his arms.

This was it, the moment he'd been avoiding his entire life. The woman he loved cried out in pain, and his baby struggled to enter the world too early. He could lose one or both of them. His legs went weak under him, but he refused to stumble, refused to fall. Fall into the pit of darkness that had surrounded him since the day he discovered she was pregnant.

No matter what, he refused to believe he'd lose Kat or

Peanut. He set her in the back seat, raced around the car, and crawled in next to her, cradling her head to his chest and stroking her hair from her face.

Each time she cried out, his gut clenched tight and he struggled to remain calm and focus on soothing Kat.

To his relief, the late hour meant no traffic, and they reached the hospital in record time. They ushered her to the maternity ward and hooked her up to machines while Wes was forced out of the way.

"Mother, you need to take deep breaths and try to relax. Your blood pressure's too high."

White blurs of walls and people spun around.

"Fetal heart rate in distress."

Words. Words of concern. Words of danger. Words of death.

Chapter Twenty Eight

PAIN. Searing, cramping, breath-stealing pain ripped through Kat's stomach and back. "Something's wrong."

Wes shoved a nurse out of the way and took her hand, brushing the damp hair from her head. "I'm here, my love. Everything's fine. I have you. The nurses have you."

"I have you," Dr. Ryland said as she entered the room. "Relax. Remember everything we talked about. We've got a plan. The baby will need to be born today since your waters broke."

"I should've stayed in bed. I shouldn't have been up and around so much."

"You did nothing wrong. This baby knows it has such amazing parents that he or she wants to meet you and just can't wait."

"So he's as patient as Kat?" Wes teased, and Kat knew he was trying to lighten the mood.

A blue paper blanket was flung over Kat and her knees

were raised. Wes stroked her head and kissed her cheek and whispered into her ear how much he loved her, his warm breath soothing her in between contractions.

"I'm afraid it's too late for an epidural, hon. I told you this baby wanted out now. You're lucky. Most new mothers are in labor for days. Someone up there is watching out for you."

She looked to Wes. "I think your mother is watching over us."

"I think you're right," he said in a choked voice.

Another sharp pain ignited from her center and wrapped around her stomach to her back. "Ohhhhhhh!"

"Don't push yet," Dr. Ryland warned. "I'll tell you when." She turned to a nurse and told her something then covered Kat's legs. "Bring in some heated blankets for Mom, please. She's cold."

Kat breathed as the contraction faded. A glass box with machines was wheeled into the room. A lamp cut on over at another table. All of it looked frightening.

"Don't you worry. These are only a precaution. The baby's heartbeat is strong. A little in distress at the moment, but I think that's because Peanut is anxious to be born." She busied herself doing something at Kat's feet behind the paper. "I assume you're not going to call the baby Peanut. What are your top contenders at the moment?"

"We have a list, everything from Charlotte to Genevieve."

"Jonathan to Barack," Wes added.

"I think when you hold Peanut, you'll know what name works." Dr. Ryland kept talking as if it were a normal day. She kept them calm, and Kat knew they'd made the right choice not to use the specialist. Sometimes a doctor with a soft touch meant more than all the years in the world of schooling.

Two hours of labor passed, and Kat thought she'd collapse at any moment. Her hip throbbed, and her muscles spasmed with weakness. "I don't know how much longer I can do this," she moaned. "I didn't know it would be this hard."

"I wish I could do this for you," Wes offered.

"No you don't, trust me," Kat teased, but another contraction took her breath and she squeezed his hand.

Dr. Ryland shot her head up over the paper and smiled. "Okay, after this contraction, take several deep breaths. On the next one, you're going to push until I say stop."

The contraction hit hard and fast and then faded. Kat took three deep breaths, and another one came right on top of that one. The sensation to push was unbearable, and she bared down.

Her breath held in a knot that matched her belly, but she didn't care because her baby would be here soon.

"Okay, one more, Kat. You've got this."

When the next contraction came on, she pushed again.

"That's it. Okay, stop pushing."

Wes kissed her head, cheek, nose. "You're doing so well, my love."

"Okay, get ready. One more big push, and your baby will be here."

She was so weak, she wasn't sure she could, but knowing their baby was right there gave her enough strength to do what she had to do so she pushed again.

"Great job. You have a beautiful baby."

Silence.

No cry. No whimper.

"Is Peanut okay?" Kat called out, her eyes growing weak and her head spinning.

"Nurse," the doctor called out.

The room erupted, and everyone closed in around her child, ushering toward the light. A light that faded. Kat clung to stay awake, to see her baby, but her eyes rolled back into her head and the world went dark.

"Our special neonatal doctor is taking a look at Peanut." Dr. Ryland said returning to below the blue paper blanket to finish working on Kat.

Her eyes slid closed and her head rolled to the side. "Dr. Ryland!" Wes's pulse hammered against his neck. "Kat!"

The heart rate monitor dinged and rang and squealed with warning.

Dr. Ryland abandoned her work and went to Kat's side. With a balled fist she rubbed her chest.

A gurgle followed by a baby's cry provided an ounce of

relief, but Wes's hands shook, his body shook...his heart shook. Kat lay lifeless in the bed.

Dr. Ryland directed the nurse to inject something into her IV, and then she told the nurse to go call another physician. "She's exhausted, and her heart took on a lot the last few weeks. I'm sure she's going to be fine, but I'm calling in a specialist to check her out."

Wes looked to the baby he had yet to meet being wheeled away and then back to Kat. His feet faced one direction, his body in another, and his heart ripped in two. He looked to Dr. Ryland.

"I promise to give you an update on Peanut in a few minutes. Stay with Kat."

He watched the doctor leave as another walked in and began assessing Kat, all while he stood by helpless. His thoughts raced. His pulse hammered. The pumping in his ears was louder than the heart rate monitor's bleep.

The monitor dinged faster. The doctor hovered over her. Nurses blocked his view. Everything spun, and he was left still in the center.

The dinging slowed, people slowed. A nurse stepped aside, and Kat's eyes fluttered open. Relief flooded him. Dots filled his vision. Dizziness spun his head until he didn't know floor from ceiling. He fell against the wall. A nurse rushed to his side.

"Sir? You okay?"

Dr. Ryland entered and knelt by his side. "It's okay, Wes. Kat and Peanut are going to be just fine. Peanut is stable and breathing independently. Mama is coming out of it."

Her words were like honey on medicine. He heaved in a breath.

"That's it. Breathe deeply." Dr. Ryland smiled at him. "You both did so great."

In that moment, he thought he could hug the woman, but instead he clawed his way up to stand.

Dr. Ryland and the nurse were immediately at his side. "Move slowly now."

Kat reached for him. "I'm okay, love." She smiled. "I had a vivid dream. A woman, she said she was your mother, told me to tell you hi."

Wes looked to the doctor. "What's in that IV?"

Kat let out an exasperated breath. "It wasn't a dream. I wanted to float away, but she pushed me back to you and Peanut."

He took hold of Kat's hand and held it to his chest. "You sure she's okay?"

"She's just fine. Her heart is recovering, and it's beating strong. We'll run more tests later, but I think Mom is exhausted, and now that baby is out, she'll recover quickly." The doctor— Wes had never even caught his name— exited, leaving Dr. Ryland, Kat, and himself in the room with one nurse.

"How's my baby? Is it a boy or a girl?"

The door opened, and in rolled a baby inside a plastic bin.

"You'll find out in just a minute." Dr. Ryland smiled

and waved over the nurse with a baby wrapped in a pink blanket.

"It's a girl?" Wes asked.

"Are you disappointed?" Kat asked.

"No, never." Wes reached for his daughter. The tiny thing could fit in the palms of his hands. "She's so tiny. Is she healthy? I mean, any known issues?"

"Based on her looks, none are apparent. We'll be running some tests but might not know for sure about developmental delays until a later time. For now, though, I can safely say she is breathing and, although she had a low Apgar at first, all seems well now." Dr. Ryland stepped away. "If you don't need anything right now, I'll leave you two to enjoy your daughter."

"Wait. There is one more thing I need." Kat twirled her engagement ring around and eyed her daughter asleep in his hands.

"What's that?"

"I know it's not in your job description, but can you help us find a minister or officiant? I want to get married right now. With our baby girl in our arms."

Wes shook his head. "Your mother's going to have a fit."

Kat shrugged, not taking her eyes off their daughter. "We'll have a formal wedding later. Right now, I want us to be family. You, me, and Allie," Kat whispered.

Wes passed his daughter into Kat's arms. Tears gushed from his eyes. He swiped them away but clung to Kat. "My mother's name? I don't remember telling you what it was."

She blinked up at him. "You didn't. My dream. She told me."

"I think I can help with that." Dr. Ryland left the room.

Wes stood there, stunned, as he tried to take in what Kat had just said. There was no other explanation. She couldn't know his mother's name any other way. Kat had met his mother. His throat tightened and he thought he could fall to the floor, but instead of giving into his fear that he had almost lost Kat, he looked down at his soon-to-be wife and their new daughter and gave silent thanks to his mother for both.

Dr. Ryland returned a few minutes later with a minister in tow. She not only delivered their child, but she stood as witness to their wedding. Their friends piled into the room, and at that moment, Wes knew the rest of his life, although no doubt full of challenges, would be the best chapter, not because he was traveling the world with Kat, but because he shared the biggest adventure of all with her. Raising their child.

Epilogue

Wes drove twenty-five miles an hour all the way home. The man had become a doting dad already.

Wind met them at their car and reached for the carrier, but Wes shook his head. "Thanks, but I've got her."

Jewels and Trevor opened the front door for them. "I can't believe it's been two weeks. You must be so happy to bring Allie home."

Wes sighed. His hair was at least half an inch longer, and he'd grown a beard. The man needed some downtime to recover from sitting in the NICU every minute of every day.

Inside, they found Trace and Dustin boxing up some floral arrangements.

Mother waited with her foot tapping. "How am I supposed to pull off your wedding next week if you aren't here to pick out flowers and taste food and cake?"

Wind clapped her hands together. "Wait, there's something more important that I want to know."

Kat raised a brow at her. "What's that?"

Wind went over to where Jewels had written on the piece of paper and placed it inside a vase. "I want to know if Jewels guessed correctly. Did you write down that they'd get married on the rooftop?"

Jewels shook her head. "Nope."

"Ha. So much for knowing all." Wind pulled out the slip of paper, unfolded it, and read the writing aloud. "Hospital room with baby."

Kat's mother gasped. "No, you didn't."

Wes slipped Allie from the carrier and walked toward her mother. "We couldn't bring home your granddaughter if we weren't married yet."

She huffed and backed away from the baby. "Nope. I'm a distant grandmother. I love from a distance, remember?"

She backed so far her legs hit the sofa and she fell back, her heels slipping out from under her. Kat couldn't help but laugh at the unladylike fall. Before she had a chance to recover, Wes placed Allie in her arms. "But we'll need respite care now and then. Who better to watch her than her grandmother?"

"I'll hire someone." Mother looked down at Allie. "She's so tiny."

Kat sat by her side. Wind dropped the paper on the table and plopped into a nearby chair. "Geesh, you wouldn't even let me carry her inside."

Her mother stroked Allie's head and kissed her hands. "You're so beautiful. I can't believe I have a granddaughter."

"Do you want me to take her back?" Kat offered.

"No." She sniffled.

Was her mom crying?

"Not for a few minutes. That doesn't mean I should be left alone with her at any point, but maybe I can help change her and feed her and stuff. When you're in the room with me, of course."

Kat leaned back and eyed all the floral arrangements. "We can discuss the wedding now if you want."

"We can do that later." Her mother cooed at Allie.

Kat noticed Wind's name written in Jewels's handwriting on the other side of the paper Wind had discarded. "Hey, what's this?"

"Oh, that's the other piece of what I know." Jewels took Trevor by the hand and moved in a little closer.

"About me?" Wind snatched it, read it, and crumbled it up in her fist. "Not funny."

"What did it say?" Trace asked, her engagement ring shining bright in the light pouring through the large windows.

Dustin chuckled. "Yeah, I want to know what has Wind blushing."

They all looked to her and then Jewels. "It says she'll get married on a stage."

Wind scowled. "Because you all think that I'm all theatrics and the only place I belong is in New York City, but what if I'm happy here? Are you saying I don't belong with all of you?"

Jewels smiled, a glint of mischief in her eyes. "I didn't say you'd get married on a Broadway stage."

Mother shushed them. "If you're going to bicker, take it outside. My granddaughter is trying to sleep."

Kat rose and slid into Wes's arms. "Trust me, Wind. If we can find happiness, so can you. And I, for one, am rooting for you and Damon." She turned to Wes and said, "You just have to have faith in love."

The End

Strawberry Amaretto Trifle

Ingredients:

- 2 quarts strawberries
- 3 tablespoons Amaretto
- 4 tablespoons sugar, divided
- 2 (8 ounce) packages cream cheese, softened
- 2 cups powdered sugar
- 1 cup sour cream
- ¼ teaspoon vanilla
- 1 angel food cake
- 1/2 pint whipping cream

- Chocolate chips or shavings

Directions:

1. Wash and cut strawberries in half in a bowl.

Add Amaretto and 3 tablespoons of the sugar and allow the mixture to sit.

2. Cream together the cream cheese, powdered sugar, sour cream, and vanilla. Set aside.
3. Whip the cream with the remaining 1 tablespoon of sugar. Fold into the cream cheese mixture.
4. Tear angel food cake into bite-size pieces and add to the cream cheese and whipping cream mixture.
5. Layer in a large bowl. Start with the berry mixture as the bottom layer and end with the berries.
6. Decorate top with a few cut strawberries and chocolate.
7. Chill before serving

Reader's Guide

1. There are not a lot of books out there for later-in-life heroines. Most traditional publishers shy away from such stories. Did you like reading about a middle-aged heroine facing a pregnancy or do you prefer younger heroines?
2. What did you think of the way Wes handled the news about Kat's pregnancy? Do you think he deserved a minute to get over the shock?
3. Do you think Kat should've told Wes about her pregnancy before she told her friends?
4. Do you think Wes was justified in resenting the Friendsters for letting themselves into Kat's place when he didn't even have a key?
5. Sometimes men need some bonding time, too. What did you think about the creation of the Mansters?
6. Kat didn't want to be anything like her own

mother because she felt neglected and unloved and judged all of her life. When she discovered why her mother behaved the way she had, she appeared to forigive her. Do you think you could've forgiven your mother so easily? Do you think she could've ever accepted her explanation before she'd faced motherhood herself?

7. Wes sold everything with a plan to spend all the time in the world with the woman he loves only to discover his life had been hijacked by an unexpected pregnancy. With nothing to distract him, he put all of his energy into caring for Kat. Do you think you would've savored the attention or resented it?
8. Wes discovered the pitfalls of health insurance and how little help many parents receive when they have a child with special needs. Were you aware of the challenges of healthcare in relation to therapeutic intervention in early childhood?
9. Do you think that you would've returned to the doctor in Summer Island and forgone the sonogram, or would you have wanted to know what to expect when the baby was born?
10. Wind's story is next. Are you excited to read the last book of the Friendsters?

Also by Ciara Knight

For a complete list of my books, please visit my website at www.ciaraknight.com. A great way to keep up to date on all releases, sales and prizes subscribe to my Newsletter. I'm extremely sociable, so feel free to chat with me on Facebook, Twitter, or Goodreads.

For your convenience please see my complete title list below, in reading order:

CONTEMPORARY ROMANCE

Friendship Beach Series

Summer Island Book Club

Summer Island Sisters

Summer Island Hope

Summer Island Romance

(Coming June 2022)

Sweetwater County Series

Winter in Sweetwater County

Spring in Sweetwater County

Summer in Sweetwater County

Fall in Sweetwater County

Christmas in Sweetwater County

Valentines in Sweet-water County

Fourth of July in Sweetwater County

Thanksgiving in Sweetwater County

Grace in Sweetwater County

Faith in Sweetwater County

Love in Sweetwater County

A Sugar Maple Holiday Novel

(Historical)

If You Keep Me

If You Choose Me

A Sugar Maple Novel

If You Love Me

If You Adore Me

If You Cherish Me

If You Hold Me

If You Kiss Me

Riverbend

In All My Wishes

In All My Years

In All My Dreams

In All My Life

A Christmas Spark

A Miracle Mountain Christmas

HISTORICAL WESTERNS:

McKinnie Mail Order Brides Series

Love on the Prairie

(USA Today Bestselling Novel)

Love in the Rockies

Love on the Plains

Love on the Ranch

His Holiday Promise

(A Love on the Ranch Novella)

Love on the Sound

Love on the Border

Love at the Coast

A Prospectors Novel

Fools Rush

Bride of America

Adelaide: Bride of Maryland

About the Author

Ciara Knight is a USA TODAY Bestselling Author, who writes clean and wholesome romance novels set in either modern day small towns or wild historic old west. Born with a huge imagination that usually got her into trouble, Ciara is happy she's found a way to use her powers for good. She loves spending time with her characters and hopes you do, too.

Made in the USA
Columbia, SC
12 October 2022